ROTTEN

BREE WILEY

CONTENTS

AUTHOR'S NOTE

I want to make it very clear that *Rotten* is a dark dystopian **HORROR ROMANCE**. While there is definitely an HEA, Charon and Hector go through some heavy situations to get there.

For your mental health, I would advise reading the Content Warning behind the Afterword in the back of the book.

In the world of 1nf3ction, seventy-six years ago scientists let loose a deadly virus into the air that started an apocalypse. Some people immediately changed into mindless monsters, and others had the infection settle into their blood, turning them into carriers. The red rain virus—RRV 13—spreads via storm system and still exists in the atmosphere. When the red rain falls, no one is safe.

Though this is book 2 in the shared world of 1nf3ction, each book is a standalone.

SOUNDTRACK

Theme Song: Fear Inoculum by Tool
Specter by Bad Omens
So Cold – Remix by Breaking Benjamin
State Of Slow Decay by In Flames
Everyone I Love Is Dead by Type O Negative
Waking Up by Ten Years
I Will Not Bow by Breaking Benjamin
My Heartstrings Come Undone by Demon Hunter
Say You'll Haunt Me by Stone Sour
Eternally Yours by Motionless In White

Date/Location: October 2025, Zone T Supermax Facility
Personnel: REDACTED
Subject: Containment Integrity - Critical Failure
Imminent

We've lost communications with the outside world months ago. Satellite pings from home base have gone dark. Damn scientists and their crazy experiments sent something biological into the air, some contagion called RRV13. It started spreading with the weather system, coming down during the red rain at random intervals. It hasn't stopped pouring in thirteen days, and we've run out of dry rations.

Half the guards are showing symptoms - blood in the eyes, skin peeling from exposure. We've executed six for biting, and not all of them turned right away.

Sometimes, the infection takes immediate control, and others, it slowly rots the host from the inside out. Unlike the biters, we can't tell who's rotten and who's not until the symptoms manifest with the rain.

Morale is gone. Sanity's not far behind.

I requested extraction two weeks ago. No response. I requested air support. Nothing.

The prisoners outnumber us, and they're adapting faster than we are. When the generators stop and the lights go out, it won't be the guards in charge anymore.

PART ONE

76 Years Later

CHAPTER ONE

T he first thing I feel when I wake up is wings.

Feathers whisper across my face gently, softer than any touch I've ever known. It makes me ache for someplace I can't remember, somewhere I might've called home, once. If it ever existed at all.

The pain is what I register next.

Burning, searing pain shooting up my leg, drawing a strangled scream from my throat as I bolt straight up—

And come face-to-face with a monster.

The Ferryman. He's enormous, bigger than any man I've ever seen. Dark strands of hair hang around his face, falling over his broad chest, biceps the size of tree trunks bunching when he crosses his arms. Cold blue eyes hold mine before darting down to my legs in anger. As I follow his gaze, another horrified scream rips out of me at the sight of a biter's teeth latched onto my ankle.

I yank my leg back before scrambling to get away, registering quickly that I'm still on his boat, surrounded by miles of red water. There are other people, too. Criminals from Aster's Hollow like me, standing as far away as possible with guns aimed at them by the soldiers surrounding us.

The sight makes me pause—a grave mistake—and the biter is on me again in seconds. It sinks its teeth into my flesh, dragging me backwards with all the strength of a newly turned infected, still resembling something human. *I fucking hate when they still look human.*

Clawing at the wood of the boat, I try to dislodge my ankle from its teeth, using my free foot to kick at its head over and over. If it were an older, rotting one, its head would cave in from my blows instantly, but this one's still fresh. Could have possibly been a woman at one point, but it's hard to tell with my blood covering its entire face.

Before I even have a chance to shake it loose, the thing wiggles its head back and forth like a dog chewing a toy, digging deeper into my flesh until bones snap.

Meanwhile, the man—the *monster*—simply stares as I struggle, his nostrils flaring when I throw out a hand toward him.

"Help!" I shriek, crawling away after managing to knock out some of the biter's teeth, but it keeps coming. Its fingers grip me with bruising force, pinning me down, and all I can do is bellow as it climbs up my body, a gaping, gory mouth coming right for my face, inches from chomping down on my cheek—

Then its head disappears from its body in a spray of blood, bouncing off the lip of the boat before landing in the water with a loud *thunk*.

"Goddammit, freak, I told you not to interfere."

The biter's body collapses onto me, fluids spurting into my mouth from the exposed neck muscles. I push it off before vomiting onto the deck.

Heavy boot steps stomp forward, and I raise my gaze in time to watch another man with an assault rifle square up to the monster.

"Your *orders* are to operate the boat," the man snarls, a good foot shorter than the giant he's trying to intimidate. He spouts off more words I don't hear as the pain in my leg starts to dissipate slowly. I can't even move it, can't even feel my foot, and as I sit up to assess the damage, more bile rises in my throat before I can stop it.

Because my foot is fucking *gone*.

Or nearly. A single string of sinew connects it to my ankle, the useless limb dragging behind me when I draw my leg up and scream into the night.

"Shut your fucking mouth." A hand cracks across my cheek so hard I fly sideways, landing against the side of the boat hard enough to dislocate my shoulder. The impact dazes me, making my head spin, but not enough to miss the monster reach out his hand and snatch the soldier by the throat.

He lifts him off the ground, the man's feet kicking wildly as he tries to free himself, his nails scratching down the monster's arms, gagging and choking for air. His neck snaps under strong fingers before his body is thrown into the river with a loud splash, and then it all goes eerily silent.

The monster watches me. And I watch him back.

Slowly, he moves forward, steps far too quiet for someone his size. I press myself into the side of the boat when he draws near. He reaches out with the hand that just killed a man, and my eyes close in relief as I *finally* welcome death to take me—

A gentle touch lands on my arm.

My lids fly open in time to see him shove my shoulder back into the socket, scowling harshly when I curse in his face.

Steely eyes meet mine briefly, something like fury and disgust flickering across his features before he raises his gaze to someone coming toward us.

"How bad is it?" A feminine voice, curt and demanding.

The monster shakes his head, lips tightening as he stands and flings a hand out at me, gesturing toward my leg. My foot.

My fucking foot that's barely connected to my body.

"Yeah, yeah, I know. He's bleeding all over your boat." Another uniformed figure kneels in front of me, this time a woman with a metallic plate covering half of her shaved head. She studies me clinically, taking in my torn clothes and the dark liquid pooling around me.

Technically, the blood loss should have killed me by now. If I were human, it would have.

A shadow descends from above, startling me with a harsh caw, and my stomach drops when a crow lands on the deck beside me.

Nyx. The Ferryman's vicious weapon.

She hops forward on bony legs, pecking once at the blood surrounding my leg with a curious head tilt. Then, in a gravelly voice that sends shivers down my spine, she croaks out one word. *"Fail."*

"Fucking rotter," the woman mutters, curling her lip in disgust. "Should have let that biter finish the job."

"Fuck you," I snarl, spitting in her face.

"Not my type," she sneers, wiping off her cheek before getting to her feet. "I prefer non-rotten dick."

Rotten. How many times have I heard that word slung at me back in Aster's Hollow? Felt it like a knife in the gut? As if being born with genes that can easily harbour the infection was *my* fucking choice.

"You hungry?" The uniformed woman smiles at the monster. "Not that he'll feed you much. He's mostly skin and bones."

Not that I'll...what?

The monster huffs, either in annoyance or excitement, I'm not sure, but nausea makes me dizzy when he steps closer. The lady's words echo in my head.

Feed him. Skin and bones.

He's going to fucking eat me.

"Stay the fuck back!" I try to shout, using my elbows for leverage to slide away.

He's kneeling above me within seconds.

There's a moment where our eyes lock, mine no doubt terrified while his gaze sizes me up like a lamb to slaughter. My pulse pounds in my ears, heart beating so fast I can't breathe as he takes my calf in one of his meaty hands. The other grasps my foot tightly, and it takes me exactly five seconds to realize what he's doing.

"No, stop, don't fucking touch me—" My words cut off in a scream when he rips my foot the rest of the way off.

Anything left in my stomach empties as burning, unbearable pain sets my nerves ablaze. A wetness spreads down my leg when my bladder releases, and I writhe in my own mess, begging for the Ferryman to carry me to death.

The world dims, my vision fading around the edges as the flames consume me, and the last thing I see before I'm ash is the flutter of crow's wings while the monster watches me die.

CHAPTER TWO

Charon

Click, click. *"Pass."*

The boat rocks beneath me from where it's tied to the dock, surrounded by red water thick with floating bodies. Some are still moving, some aren't. The price you pay for resisting.

"You all know why you're here." Jonas's voice cuts through the smoky morning air as he paces across my deck, hands clasped behind his back like he's addressing recruits instead of prisoners. I suppose in a way, he is.

Arrogant prick.

A spotlight flickers from the watchtowers overhead, casting a sickly pallor on the line of prisoners standing near razor-wire fencing. A constant reminder that Zone T was built from the bones of a prison, and it still functions like one.

I stand near the railing, Nyx perched on my shoulder, claws digging lightly through the fabric of my jacket. She shifts restlessly, black eyes glittering as she scans the row of trembling faces.

"Welcome to Zone T," Jonas continues, flashing a horrific smile that only accentuates his mutilated face. "Where freedom is earned, not given. Your crimes brought you here, and the only thing that determines your stay...is what's in your blood."

"Step forward," one of the guards commands, motioning to the next person. "Don't flinch."

A boy—sixteen, maybe—wipes his nose and glances fearfully at me, but I offer no comfort. I *can't*.

Nyx launches upward, her wings beating sharply in the air as she circles once overhead, then drops like a stone. The boy squeaks when she lands on his shoulder, stabbing her beak toward the exposed skin of his neck. A single drop of blood wells up, which she quickly laps away.

"*Pass.*"

The crowd exhales collectively, but it's short-lived when the next person is shoved forward.

Behind me, Jonas keeps talking, making me grit my teeth.

"...we must remain vigilant. The infection adapts. It hides in blood, in the water, in *everything*. But thanks to our Judge's efforts, we continue to stay ahead of the rot."

I nearly roll my eyes at the words I've heard him speak a thousand times.

Nyx flaps to the edge of the boat, already watching the next one step forward. A woman, shaking and frail. Probably hasn't slept or eaten in days, either. But it doesn't matter. Nyx will decide.

The crow lands on the woman's shoulder, then her beak comes down sharply, pecking once at the woman's throat. She flinches but doesn't move to swat the bird away.

Nyx tilts her head. "*Pass.*"

The woman sobs, and I gesture toward the gang plank, allowing her to pass where a guard waits, preparing her intake to the prison.

Next. Last one.

A man this time with darting eyes. Nyx hops to him, lightly landing on his shoulder, and the man's breath stutters when her beak meets skin.

A second passes. Then another.

Click, click. "*Fail.*"

The man starts shaking his head before the word even finishes leaving Nyx's mouth. He takes a step back, lips parting with a plea, but Nyx doesn't give him a chance to beg. She dives for his face, sharp beak piercing his eyeball, and the man shrieks when she pecks it out before swallowing the mushy mass whole.

The price you pay for being rotten.

My boat rocks violently when a soldier steps up to the man and hauls him away, his screams echoing off the high walls protecting Zone T. He'll be put with the other rotters—those who carry the infection—and sectioned off from the rest of the prisoners.

An eye for an eye.

Jonas follows them off the boat, silver glinting in the hole on his face where his nose should have been. I shudder at the thought of how painful it would be to cut off one's own nose. "Let this be a reminder to you all. Zone T is not your punishment. It's your second chance."

It's your death.

Nyx flaps back to my shoulder, talons digging into my flesh. Blood drips from her beak as she nips at my ear. "*In we go.*"

I huff, petting her head with a click of my tongue in response. *Patience.*

Rita steps up next to me, the silver plate on her skull glowing under the moonlight. "Well, that's the last of them. Except for him."

She points toward the back of the boat, where the man from earlier still lies passed out. His clothes are torn and dirty, blond curls tangled around his face. Thankfully, that leg stopped bleeding after I'd cauterized it with a hot poker.

"What shall we do with him?" she asks, tapping her chin. "Bet he'd make good sport in the pit with only one foot. Or a new test subject for the Judge."

No.

Fury lances through me, but I lift the shoulder that Nyx is on with faked disinterest, causing my bird to bristle her feathers.

Another soldier walks over to the man's prone body, kicking him hard enough in the ribs that I hear one crack, and red explodes inside my vision.

When the soldier pulls a foot back for another kick, I'm across the deck in seconds, my fist connecting with his jaw in a sickening crunch. He staggers back, spitting blood, eyes wide with disbelief.

I throw another punch, then another, until he drops like a sack of grain on my deck. The others reach for their weapons, but Rita holds up a hand, her metallic skull gleaming as she watches me.

Nyx screeches above us, landing protectively on the injured man's chest, wings spread wide. I step between them anyway, planting myself firmly over his broken body as I glare at the remaining soldiers down on the dock.

Mine.

Rita tilts her head, eyes bouncing between me and the man like she's solving a puzzle. "Got it. Don't play with the monster's food."

I bare my teeth, standing my ground as Nyx flutters to my shoulder, squawking loudly. "*In we go, in we go.*"

Rita raises a brow in amusement, stepping forward to pull two crude silver coins from her pocket. "The Judge thanks you for your service."

With a shake of my head, I wave the coins away, just wanting her off my boat so I can wrap the man's wounds.

She tilts her head. "Supply replenish?"

I nod once, and she curls her fingers around the coins before putting them away. "Until the next one, then. Get the Ferryman his supplies."

I watch as she takes the prison's new residents beyond the gates, leading them into their new life. One they never wanted, or asked for. But it doesn't matter. The Judge will soon make use of them all. Some will get the chance to become soldiers, and others, well...

Nyx shifts, her talons flexing against my jacket like she can sense my pulse quicken. I try to ignore the tightness in my chest, but my heart pounds too fast as I drag my gaze to the carrier on my deck. He's still breathing. I can see it—the slow, uneven rise and fall of his chest. Blood and dirt obscure his features, but he's alive.

"*Fail, fail,*" Nyx croaks, snapping her beak. "*Eye for an eye.*"

Shushing her sharply, I shake my head, wishing I could tell her *no, not this one.* Not those eyes.

A whistle pulls my attention toward the gates, where Jonas stands just beyond the threshold.

"Here you go, freak," he calls, grinning cruelly as he shakes a burlap ration bag. "Come and get it."

Then he's gone, vanishing behind the walls, leaving my bag on the cracked pavement *far away* from my boat.

Beyond my reach.

The water licks at the hull, whispering warnings only I can hear when I step toward the gangplank. My grip tightens on the railing, nails pressing into the damp wood as my teeth bite into my tongue. Up above, laughter erupts from the guards in the watchtowers, their weapons trained on me.

I can't leave the boat. But the bag sits there, full of everything I need to survive. And I'm starving.

Which means I have two choices:

Step onto the dock and risk whatever waits for me—death, or things worse than death.

Or stay and let the hunger hollow me out until there's nothing left.

One way or another, this boat will become my tomb.

CHAPTER THREE

Hector

"**P**retty eyes."

An eerie, scratchy voice jolts me from sleep as a weight presses down on my chest.

Cracking open an eye, I spot two beady black ones staring right back at me.

A crow. *The* crow. The Ferryman's murder bird.

My heart skips a beat. When I try to sit up, she clicks her beak sharply in warning, causing me to freeze. Her talons flex against the thin fabric of my shirt, just enough for me to feel the press of claws.

"Uh... hello?" I cough, my throat dry and raw.

"*Pretty eyes,*" she croaks loudly, feathers rustling as she cocks her head. "*Fail, fail.*"

Other than the involuntary rocking of my body, I don't dare move. The soft creak of wood reaches my ears, a faint scent of brine and old blood in my nostrils. The memory of where I am crashes into me like a wave.

The boat. I'm on a boat. And there was a monster...

I try to shift slowly, but the crow's beak snaps an inch from my face.

"Eye for an eye. Fail, fail, fail."

My head throbs enough to make me sick, ribs aching slightly. Blood coats my skin, already flaking off with each bounce of the boat. I glance away from the bird to figure out where the hell I am, scanning my surroundings.

There's a cot bolted to the wall, neatly made up with blankets, and a lantern burning low as it swings from the ceiling. The room is small, barely enough space for me on the floor, and when my eyes dart to the doorway...cold dread crawls up my spine when I realize I'm not alone.

The *monster*. A mountain in human form, standing in the doorway like a shadow. Broad shoulders fill the narrow space, arms thick and scarred, dark eyes hollowed out.

"What... the fuck," I whisper, panic cracking my voice.

He doesn't move. I can't even tell if he's breathing.

"You...you can't be human."

Still nothing.

I press back into the creaky floor as best I can, my pulse hammering so hard I can feel it in my teeth. Everyone knows the stories told of the Ferryman, how the Judge feeds him prisoners who don't cooperate, and now I'm *trapped*.

"Monster," I choke out, the word slipping free before I can stop it.

His expression falls, just barely, but still no response.

I expect rage or violence. A fight for my life as he prepares to fucking *eat me,* but...he just stands there. Watching me like a predator sizing up its injured prey. I can't even run.

Shifting my leg, I try to move my foot, but it's no longer there.

"Pretty eyes. Fail." The bird squawks loudly, making me flinch. When the giant takes one slow step forward, I scramble back, heart in my throat.

"Stay the fuck away from me!"

He lifts both hands slowly, palms out, but still doesn't talk. Just fucking *watches*. It makes my skin crawl.

As he moves again, I scoot back on my elbows until my shoulders hit the wall of the cabin, heart thundering like it's trying to punch its way out of my chest.

"Don't," I cry, my voice breaking in fear. "Please... just don't hurt me."

He freezes, a look of pain flashing across his features. And then slowly...so very slowly, he sinks onto his haunches. Making himself smaller.

His hands stay where I can see them, open and empty as he tilts his head slightly. Hair as dark as the crow on my chest falls around his shoulders. Soft blue eyes hold my gaze steady. He's... not here to hurt me. I think.

Every instinct in my body screams otherwise.

The monster taps his chest twice, then points to me, thick eyebrows raising expectantly.

I just stare at him, trembling. "What... what the hell does that mean?"

He simply repeats the gesture. Tap-tap to his chest. Points at me. But then his finger drops to my leg, and I follow it with my gaze, bracing to find a mangled, bloody stump.

Instead, I see the end of my stained pants rolled up and my ankle wrapped in heavy gauze. My brain finally catches up to what he's trying to say.

I saved you.

"What...Why? So you can eat me?"

A slow shake of his head is the only response I receive.

The bird finally hops off my chest, wings fluttering as she lands on his shoulder. "*Eye for an eye.*"

He strokes her feathers with a careful hand, all the while keeping his gaze on me.

Swallowing hard, I sit up gingerly, wincing when my ribs twinge. My entire body aches, and the severed nerve endings in my leg are starting to fire. If I were normal, if I were *human*, I would probably have gone into shock by now. Everything hurts, but once the red rain comes, I'll be as good as new.

If only I could regrow limbs.

The monster moves, making me jump, but all he does is sit cross-legged on the floor to give me space. Catching my eye, he taps his lips, then shakes his head before opening his mouth.

Can't speak.

"Shit," I mutter, dragging a shaking hand through my curls. That just makes him even more terrifying.

His large hands move to his side, where something hangs from a strap across his chest. When he pulls it over his head, the sound of liquid sloshing makes me swallow, and a small canteen appears in his grip.

Twisting the cap off, he sets it down between us on the floor, gently pushing it toward me. An offering.

My mouth goes bone-dry, head still swimming, and I can taste the copper of blood at the back of my throat, but I don't move. There's no telling what's in there, and I've seen many a poor soul fall victim to contaminated water.

He nudges it forward again, just an inch, then sits back with his palms raised as the crow clicks her beak from his shoulder.

"*Good to go,*" she croaks demonically.

I just stare at the canteen like it's a snake poised to strike.

After a moment, the monster scoffs before slowly reaching for it, keeping his eyes on my face. He takes a sip himself, just a small one, before setting it down again on the floor. Waiting.

I lick my cracked lips, so fucking thirsty I feel like I'm dying.

He leans back, giving me more space, never breaking eye contact as he crosses his thick arms.

Finally, I reach out, snatching the canteen so fast I nearly drop it before bringing it to my mouth.

The water is warm and slightly off, but it's the best thing I've ever tasted. I damn near drain the entire thing before I can stop myself. A few drops dribble onto my chin, and I swipe them up quickly, licking the remnants off the back of my hand. Due to the red rain, water sources are scarce, and creeks are no longer safe. Either you work up enough tokens in the mines to get rations from the Judge, or you die.

When I look up, the monster is watching me with an odd expression. Heat creeps up my cheeks at my desperation, but I simply wipe my mouth before handing the canteen back. "Uh... thanks."

He nods once.

Letting out a slow breath, I roll my aching shoulders, feeling vulnerable once again. I turn my head to study the room with clearer vision before glancing at him sideways.

And he's still staring. So is that damned bird.

"What do you want with me? Why am I here and not in *there?*"

I point toward the door, not entirely sure which direction Zone T lies, but he seems to understand what I'm saying.

Reaching into his pocket, he pulls out some kind of folded sack before unfurling it on the floor between us. Big, bold letters printed in red run across the middle of it, and he points at them before pointing at me.

RATIONS.

Though I can't read, I've seen this bag before. Everyone has. Just because the Judge sits inside Zone T doesn't mean he has no control over the surrounding outposts, too. Many of us have *died* for those rations. Food, medicine, water. Shit we need to survive, yet he only has his soldiers deliver them when he sees fit.

Kiss their boots, die inside Zone T, or starve to death. Those are your only options this far north.

"What does this mean?" I ask, the thought of food making my stomach twist. "You want me to... get rations for you?"

He nods quickly, something like hope sparking on his features, but I scoff as I gesture down to my leg. "How am I supposed to do that when you ate my fucking *foot?*"

The light in his eyes dims, and he drops his head, chest heaving on an exhale. He stays like that for a long moment, desperation radiating off him in waves.

I almost feel bad. Almost.

But then he lifts his head again, and when his eyes meet mine, they're hard as steel. He taps his chest once, then points at me before curling his fingers into a fist.

When I just stare, unsure of what to make of him, he huffs and tries again, this time thumping his chest before pointing at my leg, whispering so low I can barely hear him. But I read his lips just fine.

"Owe me."

"You've got to be fucking kidding." A humorless laugh bursts from my lungs. "For saving me? You and those freakshow soldiers are the ones who hurt me in the first place!"

His expression doesn't change, but his damned bird clicks her beak.

"Eye for an eye," she squawks again. *"Fail."*

"You think saving my life means I'm yours to do with as you please?"

He nods, mouthing one word. *"Mine."*

I just sit there, glaring at him, bile rising in my throat.

He stares for a long, heavy moment before slowly reaching for the ration sack again, like he's afraid I'll startle if he makes any sudden movements. His fingers trace the bold red letters as he turns it toward me and taps it twice.

Then he points to me.

And then... to himself.

Back and forth.

You. Me. You. Me.

Then he mimics breaking something in half.

I frown, trying to decipher what he's saying. "You're... splitting them with me?"

He nods again, a flash of blue sparking in those deep irises.

I swallow hard, my throat suddenly tight. All my life, it's been scraps. Take what you can, keep it for yourself, and hide the rest. Survival of the hungriest. Eat or be eaten.

And here's this monster—this giant of a man with haunted eyes—offering half his rations to me like it's no big feat.

Letting out a shaky breath, I rub my eyes dazedly. "Why? You could just force me to do it. Threaten me."

What the fuck am I saying?

The monster only shakes his head slowly, glacial eyes searching my face.

I glance down at my mangled leg, sorting through the thoughts in my head. Rations come from inside the zone, and I need to get in there anyway. If I agree to help him, even if it's just a farce, and he gets me inside the walls...well, I'm not above lying to get what I need. But he did wrap my ankle for me.

My gaze drags back to his, still watching me unnervingly. "If I say no, you're not going to eat the rest of me, right?"

For a brief moment, the corners of his mouth twitch. Not quite a smile, but close. He shakes his head again.

I hate this, I hate *him*.

I hate that I owe him.

And I hate the Judge and those fucking soldiers for putting me in this situation.

But just like every day since the day I was born, I don't have a choice.

Eat or be eaten.

"Fine," I groan, dragging a hand through my greasy curls. The monster's face lights up with relief under the glow of the lantern swinging above. His cheeks brighten in color, almost as pink as a sunset.

Most of all, I hate how I notice that, too.

CHAPTER FOUR

Charon

H e's too thin.

The torn shirt hangs from his frame, revealing bony shoulders and a prominent collarbone. His eyes—a vibrant emerald, like the forest foliage after a clear rain—are sunken in, with dark bruises surrounding the sockets and hollowed-out cheeks. He looks no different than most of the people in the surrounding outposts, and yet... this is the first time I actually feel guilty for it.

He clearly knows more about starving than I do.

When he tries to stand, using the wall for leverage, his arms tremble as he cries out in pain. I immediately stand to help, reaching for him, but he quickly slaps my hand away with a snarl.

"Don't touch me." Those gorgeous eyes blaze with fire, a juxtaposition to his fragile appearance. Just like they did when the soldiers shoved him onto my boat yesterday. My heart thumps wildly with the urge to claim that fire for myself.

"So what's the plan?" he asks, chest heaving from exertion as he steadies himself on one leg. "Am I just supposed to... hop right into Zone T and *ask* for some rations or some shit?"

I shake my head quickly, beckoning for him to follow before turning on my heel. The ceilings are low in the cabin, and I duck into the narrow hallway, almost making it to the galley before I realize he isn't behind me. Harsh breathing reaches my ears.

When I turn back around, I spot him through the doorway, struggling to move. His leg trembles beneath him, body shaking with the effort to stay upright. The doorframe creaks under the grip he's using to keep himself from collapsing.

He won't make it far like that.

Moving into the galley, Nyx flutters off my shoulder as I grab a folding chair next to the counter. It's made of cheap, weathered plastic, beaten all to hell, but the steel legs are solid.

When I return, the man is still gripping the wall, muttering curses under his breath. Those golden curls stick to his neck, enticing me to run my fingers through them and tug.

Instead, I set the chair in front of him, not offering to help or touch, just...giving him something he can choose.

A crutch without shame.

He blinks at it, breathing hard. "...Seriously? A chair?"

I meet his gaze with a shrug. *Better than nothing.*

Huffing in annoyance, he wraps both hands around the back, using it for balance. It screeches a bit as he leans into it, his good foot dragging when he starts to move painfully slow.

But forward.

I follow behind when he passes by, not too close to scare him.

"This is ridiculous..." he grumbles, scooting down the hall. "Might as well just eat me, there's no way I can run from a biter like this."

Nyx chitters somewhere above, like she's laughing at him, and he stops suddenly to take in my small galley.

It's cramped, barely more than a closet with a sink. The walls are stained with salt and old grease, patched over by mismatched sheet metal or scrap I bartered. A single porthole filters in pale light, casting everything in a grayish glow.

Cabinets hang open, their hinges long since rusted out, filled with cans stripped of labels and whatever dried goods haven't molded yet. A fold-down table sits bolted to the opposite wall, stained with oil.

"This is where you *live*?" he asks incredulously.

I just shrug and start toward the narrow staircase that leads up to the deck.

The boat isn't pretty, but it's home. It's all I have left, besides Nyx.

Behind me, the man mutters, "He's definitely going to fucking eat me."

I pretend not to hear that, my stomach revolting at the thought of consuming human flesh.

The stairs groan under my weight as Nyx flutters ahead, slipping through when I open the hatch. I reach the top and step aside, holding the heavy wooden door open.

He drags the chair forward, one stubborn scoot at a time, jaw clenched. Every step looks like it costs him a tremendous amount of energy, but still, he doesn't ask for help. And I don't offer.

Hauling himself up the stairs with the chair in one hand, he finally spills out onto the deck, blinking against the lights shining from Zone T's walls. "Well. That sucked."

I point straight ahead, across the cracked and weedy expanse of shoreline to the rations bag beyond my reach.

Bright red letters, obnoxiously obvious. Just sitting there like bait, abandoned near the gate of the prison's outer wall.

He follows my finger, groaning loudly when he sees it. "Oh, come on."

His gaze bounces from the bag to the gates, then back at me, like maybe this is a joke. Like maybe I'll laugh and tell him I'm just kidding.

I'm not.

"You want me to go out there?" he whispers fiercely, green eyes wide. "With one foot and a fucking chair?"

I dip my chin once in confirmation.

His nostrils flare. "Why the hell can't *you* get it?"

Tapping my chest, I point to the towers beyond the gates, and then at the floor, shaking my head. *I can't leave the damned boat.*

He lets out a frustrated growl. "I don't understand what the fuck you're saying, but I think I get it. I'm expendable and you're not, right? I'm just pathetic and slow and obviously dying, so why not send me as bait?"

I shake my head adamantly, pointing once again at the towers, *desperately* trying to get my point across.

"You know what's gonna happen if they see me, right? They won't warn me. They'll shoot on sight or feed me to the fucking pit. I can't fight off a biter with one foot!"

His chest heaves as he hyperventilates, but I let him burn it out because he's right to be mad. I wouldn't risk him if I had any other choice. *I'd rather die than him.*

When he falls quiet again, I crouch down, tapping the railing gently to get those pretty eyes back on me. His gaze meets mine, pupils blown wide in fear as I show him the crossbow leaning against the side of the boat, mouthing, *"I've got you."*

He stares at me, jaw clenched tight. "And what if I don't make it?"

Thumping my chest before shaking my head, I hold his gaze steady, begging him to trust me. I won't let him die. Not if I can help it.

He doesn't say anything for a long moment, just squints at the gates in the distance, scanning the towers. "Do they know you're out here?" When I nod, he swears under his breath, his fingers tightening around the chair. "I don't know how I'm supposed to do this. Just...hobble over there, snatch the bag, and hobble back?"

Lifting the crossbow to my shoulder, I jerk my chin toward the gangplank for him to proceed, earning me a grimace and a hard swallow. I dip my gaze to his pink lips before looking away, keeping my eyes on the prize.

Finally, after a moment's hesitation, he starts toward the ramp. "You better keep your fucking promise, monster. I'm not dying for you."

I don't react, just watch him slowly move toward the dock like a wounded animal. Little does he know that I always keep my promises. Always.

There are far too many ghosts haunting me to let one more person die.

CHAPTER FIVE

Hector

This wasn't the fucking plan.

The chair wobbles every time I shift my weight, fire shooting up what's left of my leg. My foot—or lack thereof—throbs with every heartbeat, my palms slick with sweat.

The bag sits maybe fifty yards away. Might as well be across the entire continent at the pace I'm moving. Goddammit, I was supposed to get *into* Zone T, not outside of it.

Glancing back at the boat, I catch the monster's silhouette on deck, all muscle and shadow, watching me with those unnervingly calm eyes. Crossbow aimed and at the ready.

His protection and willingness to keep watch should make me feel safe.

All I feel like is an easy target.

A cold wind picks up, carrying the scent of rust and something very, very *wrong*. I tighten my grip on the chair, dragging it across the uneven dock until the wood gives way to cracked earth and weeds. Every scoot forward fills me with dread.

My good leg screams from the effort, and my arms ache from bearing all my weight. The chair rattles over broken ground, nearly echoing off the prison walls. I swear a biter could hear this shit from a mile away. Or worse, one of the soldiers operating the towers up above.

As the wind shifts again, bringing with it a faint whisper of sound, I freeze, listening. One glance over my shoulder tells me nothing is there but moss and filthy water—no movement of any kind. But I swear I heard *something*.

The monster raises one fist, holding it steady, the gesture clear as day. *Halt. Stop. Hold.*

Ignoring him, I grit my teeth and press forward, every instinct screaming to turn back, but that bag is *right there*. I'm going to get it even if I have to crawl and drag myself back.

Truth be told, I'm fucking hungry, and that freak with the murder bird is the only thing between me and starvation. Plus, I'm starting to think he might actually care if I live, which is confusing all on its own.

I'm maybe five feet from the bag when my arms finally start to go numb. My breath shoots from my lungs, sweat pouring down my neck despite the chill. And the rations are *so close*.

"Gotcha," I mutter, dragging the chair one last time before I collapse to my knees with a grunt. My fingers fumble for the strap, barely curling my hand around it, relief making me dizzy, and—

CRACK.

The ground explodes beside me, dirt spraying up into my face, dazing me. My ears ring from the sound of a gunshot.

CRACK. CRACK.

Two more shots. One slams into the chair beside me, sending a shockwave through my skull.

"*Fuck!*" I yell, throwing myself flat, clutching the bag to my chest like a shield as my heart pounds against my chest.

I can't run, I can't crawl. I'm *completely exposed.*

"Dance, rotter, dance!" One of the soldiers in the tower laughs, mocking me as he lets loose another bullet.

I twist just enough to look back at the boat, screaming for help, but the monster doesn't move. He's off the railing now, crouched low, every muscle tensed like he wants to run, but he *doesn't.*

And now I'm completely fucked.

The bag presses tight against my chest as I start crawling toward the dock, another bullet hitting the ground close by. Pain lights up every nerve in my body, my mangled leg dragging behind like dead weight. My elbows scrape raw on the concrete, but I don't stop. The monster's still watching me, eyes locked, tracking every inch I drag myself.

A bullet whistles past my head and I scream through my teeth, adrenaline the only thing keeping me moving. I've just about reached the dock when a strangled cry reaches my ears from the water's edge. My eyes snap to the side, and I freeze in terror.

A biter crawls from the water, half its torso gone, the remains bloated and black with rot. Seaweed tangles through its ribs, barnacles clinging to what's left of its spine. The thing hauls itself onto the dock with ruined hands, leaving a smear of entrails in its wake as it shudders toward me, gurgling, eye sockets empty.

I choke on my own breath, gaze darting between the gangplank and the decaying creature clawing its way closer. *Fuck, fuck.* The biter snarls, jaws unhinging with a sickening pop as it lunges—

Thwack.

Its head snaps forward violently, a wooden bolt jutting from the middle of its skull. The body jerks once, then collapses in a wet heap inches from my face, black sludge oozing from the wound.

I gasp, staring in disbelief when the corpse twitches once more before it goes completely still. A sharp clack echoes across the dock, and I lift my head to spot the Ferryman at the edge of the boat, crossbow still raised. His hair whips across his face wildly, furious eyes locked onto mine as he waves me forward quickly.

Yanking the bolt from the biter's head, I shove it back into the river and continue to scoot toward the gangplank, only a foot away. I've just about crawled onto it when another gunshot cracks through the air, *ripping the bag from my arms.*

Twisting, I roll to my side just in time to see a hole tear clean through the ration sack, and *everything*—packets of dried food, herbs, bandages—spills over the gangplank into the contaminated waters below. Bleeding out like guts.

"No!" I scream, watching it all wash away with the current. "*No, no, no.* Fuck!"

Scrambling to gather up what I can, another bullet hits the dock right next to my head, kicking up dust into my eye. The monster shouts, not with words, but a guttural, raw growl from the boat that has my hair standing on end.

He's halfway up the mast now, pulling something down, an old tarp that'll give me a second of cover. I shove what's left of the rations into my shirt and crawl, dragging myself up. Nyx screeches overhead like a banshee, swooping through the air like she's trying to draw fire.

I don't know how the hell I make it up the gangplank, but I do, and when my fingers scrape the deck, when I feel the boat rock beneath me, I *sob*. I bawl. I don't stop moving until the Ferryman hauls me up with shaking hands and drags me into his arms.

I collapse against his chest, the half-shredded bag crumpled between us, torn open like a corpse. Everything's ruined. Everything's gone, and I can't breathe. I can't look at him.

I almost died, and the monster saved me *again*.

CHAPTER SIX

Charon

I couldn't do anything.

The table creaks under my weight as I rest my head in my hands, heart still pounding from watching what's *mine* nearly die again. Each bullet that came close to embedding in his skull ripped open old wounds, harsh memories, and once again, I was left *helpless*. Unable to intervene. Trapped.

I shouldn't even care about him. Losing those rations should be more important, not the life of some rotter I met yesterday, and yet those eyes...The thought of witnessing those eyes close forever makes me nauseous. I can't go through that again. I won't survive it a second time.

The bathroom door groans on its hinges. I glance up to find him peeking out at me, curls damp from the small bucket of water I offered him to clean up with. He uses the door jamb to hop out, dressed in a fresh pair of my clothes, the trousers rolled up over his mangled ankle. They're far too big on his thin frame, but at least they aren't covered in dirt and blood. From now on, my clothes are his.

He steadies himself against the table, taking in the bowl of soup I made for him before meeting my gaze, and I'm struck senseless by the sight of his unsoiled skin. It looks so... soft, for how tight it stretches over his cheekbones. Frail. As delicate as bird wings.

"Is this all you have to eat?" he asks, collapsing into a seat across from me, and I nod toward the jars of preservatives in the cupboard. There's enough to last me at least another week, but... not with two mouths to feed.

He stares down at the soup for a long moment before glancing up at me suspiciously. "What's in this? It's not my foot, is it?"

My lips twitch, but I shake my head, pointing once again to the pickled vegetables.

"You eat it." He shoves the bowl toward me and snarls when I try to push it back. "Eat it. We both know I can survive longer without food than you can."

I blink, realizing he has a point. Rotters don't need to eat as much as the rest of us do, but he looks so pale and he lost a lot of blood. So I tighten my jaw and scoot the bowl toward him firmly, giving him my no-nonsense look that I haven't used in years. I'd whisper, but my shout from earlier completely wrecked my throat.

It seems to be effective, anyway.

The man huffs, grabbing the wooden spoon before taking a bite of cabbage. His eyes close momentarily, a slight noise in the back of his throat telling me that he likes the taste. I wish I could tell him not to hold back, to let me hear every noise from those full lips. When he opens them again, they drag over my torso as he takes another spoonful.

"Are those bites?" he asks, gesturing to the scars on my arms.

I nod once, and his brows jump beneath his curls.

"So you're immune to the infection, then?"

Another nod from me as I shift my shoulders uncomfortably, fighting the urge to hide my arms.

He continues to eat, his gaze scanning the galley before landing back on me. "Why did you need those rations so badly? What happens when you run out of food?"

All I can do is stare at him, because the answer should be obvious. What happens to all of us when we starve? We die.

"You can't just get more from Zone T? I thought you were the Judge's lap dog or something? They call you Charon, the Ferryman."

Scrubbing a hand down my face, I shake my head, gesturing around the boat.

The man growls in frustration. "I don't understand what you're trying to tell me!" he snaps, throwing his spoon into the half-empty bowl.

Desperation pinches my chest. I could *tell him,* but I can't. I just point at the grotesque scar across my throat before pointing toward the prison, pleading for him to *hear me.*

His gaze bounces between my neck and finger, still not understanding. "And you couldn't leave the boat to get those rations because...?"

I jerk my thumb toward Zone T again, to the watchtowers.

They'll kill me if I step on land.

The man grabs his spoon again, frowning when he takes another slow bite. "So we're trapped here. Both of us."

My shoulders sag as I give him a tight nod.

"Whatever you did to piss off the Judge must have been really bad."

It was so much more than that, but I have no way of communicating, nothing to write with, and I don't feel like reliving those horrors again. So I just watch him eat. Watch the way his lips plump up with each bite, his throat flexing with each swallow. Thin, bony fingers curled around the spoon. It's fascinating to me how fragile he looks, and yet there's so much strength in those eyes. I want them trained on me, and only me, forever.

The silence stretches on, my boat creaking around us until he finishes, and he wipes his mouth on his sleeve before pushing away the bowl. Then he finally gives me what I want, meeting my gaze. "I'll do it. Once I'm healed enough, I'll... get your rations. Somehow."

My brows slam down as I tilt my head in confusion, but he runs his fingers through his hair with a shrug. "You've saved my life twice now. I owe you."

I shake my head adamantly because he almost *died* repaying me, but the man just holds up a hand. He pushes to a stand with a grunt, swaying slightly before catching himself on the edge of the table. I rise halfway from my chair, ready to catch him should he fall, but he glares at me until I sit back down.

"This is my choice," he says firmly. "I don't like having debts. Once it's paid, I'm gone."

I study him while he breathes through clenched teeth, clearly still in pain.

Gone. I should be glad for it, shouldn't I? It's hard enough surviving on my own out here, let alone having someone else to look after, but he's mine. He's not going anywhere without me, and since I can't leave, neither can he. My decision is final.

The man rubs the back of his neck, eyes scanning the cramped galley like he's looking for something. "...Where am I supposed to sleep?"

Blinking, I pause for a moment, caught off guard. It would be preferable if he slept in my bed, but the man is stubborn and I know he'd refuse at first. There's time enough for that, anyway.

I motion with a dip of my chin, then push away from the table and lead him slowly through the narrow hallway. Past the cot where I sleep, past the storage room, to a small bench tucked away in the far corner of the cabin. It's not much, just a thin blanket and a lumpy pillow, but it's warm. Dry. Safe.

He eyes it cautiously before swinging his gaze over to me. "Your name," he says slowly. "It *is* Charon, right?"

I offer him another nod.

"Right. Of course it is. Big, broody, cannibal Charon. The fucking feet eater."

That one earns the slightest tilt of my mouth.

Looking down, he wiggles his bare toes against the wooden floor, his voice softer when he speaks again. "...I'm Hector."

And with that, he hops over to the bench, lowering himself down slowly. He flops onto his side, facing away from me, no more words spoken. Just the quiet creak of the boat and the whistle of wind outside.

Turning around, I walk back down the hall toward my cot and lie down, stretching out my aching legs as I reach into my nightstand and carefully pull out the book I've read every night of my life for the past thirty-four years. His name runs through my head on a loop, the soft way it sounds, syllables I can easily pronounce.

"Hector," I whisper, running my hand over my book's ragged cover, the name familiar in my mouth and kind on my damaged vocal cords. Then I say it again, testing the feel on my tongue.

And for the first time in almost a decade, I don't mind the silence pressing in on me as I drift off to sleep, because someone else is breathing under this roof with me. Not quite next to me, yet, but...

For tonight, that's all I need.

CHAPTER SEVEN

Hector

"I'll come back for you."

She'd promised, holding my hand over her heart as she tucked my curls behind my ear. *"Hector, be strong. I'll come back."*

"But where are you going?" I'd asked, barely ten years old, already no stranger to life's cruelty.

She adjusted the pack across her back, avoiding my gaze as she'd glanced around the shack we'd been living in since Father left. *"Zone T, to join the soldiers. They need to know the truth."*

"What truth? How long will you be gone?" I remember feeling panicked, not of being alone, but of being left behind. Being forgotten.

My sister had ruffled my hair before giving me one last hug. *"Don't get into trouble and stay out of the woods. Soldiers are pa-*

trolling the trails. You should have enough supplies stocked up until I return. I love you, little brother."

And then she'd walked away.

That was ten years ago.

The food had run out after a month, the water after a few weeks.

I was alone. I was rotten. And I knew nothing but pain.

The bench creaks beneath me as I jolt awake. My heart pounds in my chest. Bright light bleeds through the porthole, casting the room in a dusty glow that has me sneezing when I sit up slowly.

It's been... years since I had that dream. Being so close to Zone T—to *her*, hopefully—must have set it off.

Pain flares up my calf, muscles and nerves spasming enough to make me whimper, but I bite it back before the sound leaves my lips. I'm not used to feeling so much. Shoving the blanket off, I swing my good leg over the edge and rub my sleep-crusted eyes.

The silence around me is thick. I prick my ears, listening beyond the boat's interior, but all I hear is the rush of running water outside.

The monster—Charon—isn't here. At least not in the cabin.

With a groan, I pull myself to a stand, all of my joints stiff from the ordeal yesterday. Using the wall as leverage, I slowly hop down the hallway, pausing at his room to double-check that he's not here. His cot is empty, covers neatly made. Almost like he didn't sleep in it at all. The small kitchen is also empty, but the doors leading to the deck are flung open, allowing the midday sun to spill in. I must have slept longer than I thought.

Curiosity gets the better of me, and I use the opportunity to poke around after scrubbing the sleep from my face in the bathroom, starting with the monster's—I mean, *Charon's* room first.

It's minimal at best. I didn't get a good chance to look at it last night, but in the light of day, it seems quite plain. Not at all what I expected. No bones or blood, no corpses in the corner. Just a patched-up coat hanging on a hook and a nightstand bolted to the wall with a single drawer.

A drawer that's partially open...

I shouldn't. I should turn around and go back to my bench, or scrounge the cabinets for something to eat. Go find the giant man and his murder bird. Definitely shouldn't be reaching for the drawer with shaky hands, slowly pulling it open to reveal a single, water-damaged book inside. Its spine is falling apart, the cover too faded to reveal the title, but I stare at it in awe, too afraid to touch.

Books are *rare*. I've never so much as seen one in my life, but I've heard stories of them from before the rains came. Before the infection, when people had copious amounts of time to immerse themselves in stories instead of fighting every day to survive. It almost sounds like a fairytale.

As far as I know, Aster's Hollow had burned all of their books decades ago to keep the bellows operating for silver production.

Where did he get it? What's it about? Can he read? I only know the word *rations* because it's on the bags we all fight over. Who taught him? Where did he—

A creak in a floorboard has me slamming the drawer shut, pulse in my ears as I spin around. Charon's large frame fills the doorway, blocking out all light.

"Fuck, I…" My voice cracks. "I was just looking."

He remains still, and the silence feels like being caught robbing a grave under his heavy gaze—no response of any kind.

That's somehow worse than reacting.

I wave vaguely toward the nightstand, sweat forming on the back of my neck. "I didn't take anything. I just saw the book. That's all."

Charon tilts his head slightly, not in anger, but more… curious. His expression doesn't seem as harsh as it looked last night in the dark. There's a tilt to his lips that's almost a smile. It eases me slightly.

"Where'd you get it?" I ask, nodding toward the drawer. "The book, I mean. I've never seen one before."

He blinks before stepping into the room, softly walking toward me. I hop out of the way when he draws closer, watching him reach into the drawer to pull it out. The way he handles it is gentle, turning it over in his hands with a tenderness that makes my heart lurch, and then opens the first few pages before holding it out to me.

I take it slowly, carefully, because it looks like it might fall apart in my hands. The pages are warped, ink smudged in places. He points to something written in the corner, but I just stare at the words, at how many there are. So many symbols on the page.

It's overwhelming.

"I can't read this shit," I mutter, shaking my head as I hand it back to him.

Charon's shoulders slump, something sad flashing in his eyes as he takes it from me and sets it back in the drawer. He almost looks devastated.

Fuck, I wish I could read, if only to wipe that look off his face. It's... I don't like it.

A beat of silence passes between us before he straightens, motioning me to follow. I take a moment to collect myself before I move, casting one last glance at the drawer when I go.

He's waiting for me at the top of the stairs, patiently silent while I crawl on my hands and knees up to the deck. When I finally get up there, raising my eyes to the bright sunlight hitting my irises, I gasp at the view surrounding us.

It's like stepping into a dream.

To our left, a waterfall spills from jagged rocks above, frothing as it crashes into the river below. Mist hangs in the air, splitting the light into shards of color. The boat sits along the riverbank under a cropping of trees, their leaves a soft green that glows in the sun. Clusters of red berries hang from their branches, a burst of blood against vibrant emeralds.

The water from the falls is nearly transparent, and for the first time in what feels like forever, there's no rot. No decay. No stench of death or iron in the air. My eyes start to sting as I take it all in, afraid that if I blink, the scene will disappear. It's unlike anything I've ever seen before. When I turn to Charon, he's already watching me with a soft expression.

"What is this place?"

He simply nods his head toward one of the low-hanging branches above us before pointing to a bucket on the deck, half-filled with berries. My heart drops right through the floor.

When he stretches up, plucking one free before popping it into his mouth like it's no big fucking deal, all the blood drains from my body.

"*No!*" I grab his jaw in one hand while my other attempts to invade his mouth. "Spit it out, spit it out!"

He flinches and stumbles back a step as my fingers jab at his face, desperate to dislodge the berry he just casually ate.

"Do you want to die?!" I shout, fingers still prying. He lets out a muffled grunt. "Charon, spit it out, you *absolute* lunatic—"

He grabs my wrists firmly, holding me in place as he opens his mouth and sticks out his tongue to show me that the berry is gone. *Swallowed.* I'm too late.

I jerk free from his grip, backing away as though *I've* been poisoned. "What the *fuck* is wrong with you? We don't eat things, hasn't anyone ever told you that?!"

My arms start to tremble, a cold sweat breaking out along my spine, because all I can see in my mind is him convulsing on the deck, frothing at the mouth, *leaving me behind when he dies,* and—

Thunk.

Something small and wet hits the deck beside us, drawing my attention momentarily from my racing thoughts. I glance down to find another berry at my feet. Then another.

Thunk. Thunk.

Nyx sits on the railing just above, her head cocked sharply to the side. She flutters her wings once. "*Pass. Good to go.*"

I freeze, gaping up at her before slowly turning toward Charon. He raises an eyebrow at me, lips tilted in amusement. Nyx casually hops down to the deck and pecks at one of the berries, her beak stained red.

"Are you fucking kidding me?" I growl, dragging a hand down my face. "How is this even possible?"

The plant life is contaminated, the animals are contaminated. *Everything* is contaminated! At least, that's what the Judge has told us. Otherwise, rations wouldn't be such a commodity.

Charon just shrugs, plucking another berry off the branch before holding it out toward me in his palm.

I hesitate, hard. But he doesn't move, just stands there quietly, his eyes locked on mine like he's asking me to trust him.

And, fuck, I think I do. Tentatively—*very* tentatively—I take it from him and sniff it. Hold it like it'll kill me, because until this exact moment, I believed it would.

"*Pass,*" Nyx squawks again, hopping a few inches closer. "*Good to go.*"

"Yeah, yeah, I heard you."

Fuck it. I toss the berry into my mouth, moaning in surprise when a burst of flavor explodes on my tongue. It's sweet and tart. *Alive.* My stomach clenches with hunger so sharp it almost drops me to my knees.

Charon's watching me again, not smiling—he never really smiles—but there's something heated in his gaze as I reach down and grab two more from the bucket, popping them both into my mouth with another moan.

Nyx croaks approvingly and flutters to the railing again like she's pleased with herself.

I swallow down the fruity goodness, licking juice from my thumb. "Alright, fine. These aren't dangerous, but I don't understand how. I thought the rain infected everything."

Charon drops his gaze to my mouth before turning away, shrugging again as he continues to pick berries. He must have already been at it for a while, because there's not much more within reach. Once he's gotten all he can, he wipes his hands on his pants and frowns down at the bucket. It's still not full.

An idea pops into my head.

"I can help," I say before I can stop myself, feeling a little silly when he gives me a blank look. "The ones that are higher up. I can grab them, just... put me on your shoulders."

He rears back, eyes widening like I just said something ridiculous.

"I'm serious. We could probably fill the bucket if I got the rest. Let me help."

God knows why I want to help, but I do.

Charon looks from me to the branches, then back again. His lips press into a thin line and for a second, I think he's going to flat-out refuse. But then he sighs through his nose and shakes his head, crouching down in front of me.

I blink at him in shock for a moment. "Wait, really?"

He doesn't answer, just reaches out, grabs my wrist, and hauls me onto his shoulders like I weigh nothing.

"Shit!" I let out a startled yelp, grabbing onto his head for balance. "Okay, fuck, how about a warning next time?"

He stands slowly, keeping me balanced with an iron grip around my legs.

From up here, the world looks... different. Calmer. I reach up and start plucking berries, dropping them into the bucket below as Nyx circles lazily overhead, cawing every so often.

"You're surprisingly stable," I murmur after a while, trying not to knee him in the face accidentally. "Like a really quiet horse. Or a donkey."

He makes a noise in his throat that might be disapproval. Or laughter. Either way, I chuckle softly, feeling freer with this stranger than I probably should. His fingers tighten on my thighs, and the silence that follows is almost... comfortable. Peaceful.

I let my hand rest lightly on the top of his head, just for a moment, before continuing to drop berries into the bucket. For once, I even ignore the instinct in my gut telling me to watch out for danger.

Maybe, with the Ferryman looking after me...I don't have to.

CHAPTER EIGHT

Charon

He let me touch him.

That's all I can think about as I direct the boat closer to the fresh waterfall, turning us port side until the bow passes just below the current.

He let me touch him, and he touched me. My palms still tingle from the feeling of his warm thighs beneath them. Does this mean he's no longer scared of me? Does he trust me?

My chest tightens painfully at the thought of how much I want that.

Water cascades onto the boat, soaking the floor before draining beneath the railing. Letting go of the tiller, I head toward a group of barrels near the railing and start filling one up, keeping Hector in my periphery as he gazes at the sunset glittering off the river. His curls blow gently in the wind, covering his brow, and he brushes them away with a somewhat wistful expression. I wonder what he's thinking about. I wish I could tell him everything on my mind.

Nyx caws on my shoulder, causing him to snap his attention toward us, and he uses the railing for balance as he hops over. He needs something to help get around. I glance at the branches I've gathered near the cabin doors, hoping to rectify that for him tonight.

"Is this for drinking?" he asks, gesturing toward the barrel.

I nod before mimicking the act of eating with my hands. *Drinking and eating.*

His nose scrunches, accentuating the freckles dotting his cheeks as he studies the tinted water. "It's clearer than the pond near Aster's Hollow, I suppose, but you'll still have to sterilize it."

I simply nod again, watching him closely. Something about his expression enthralls me and I can't make heads or tails of it. Maybe it's because he's small, yet fierce, like an alley cat. Or maybe it's because I'm surrounded by the Judge's soldiers who mutilate themselves for fun. Either way, Hector is... pure. Whole.

Well. Minus the foot.

When the barrel begins to overflow, I reach for the next one, turning back in time to watch him try to push the full one out of the way. He grunts, almost falling over when he uses too much force, and I wrap my arm around his waist to hold him steady.

"Fucking hell," he mutters, slipping out of my grasp. His eyes scan six more. "You're filling *all* of these?"

I dip my chin and point to Zone T in the distance, far enough away that its towers are barely visible above the tree line, hoping he understands.

Hector's eyes darken when he follows my finger. "You're doing this for *them.* The soldiers and the Judge." There's an accusatory tone to his voice that rankles me. "How often?"

I hold up three fingers, for three times a month, but I'm not sure if he understands.

He glares down into the rapidly filling barrel for a quiet moment. "Why would you do that? He hurts people like me. Why are you helping him?"

All I can do is stare, because how can I begin to explain without words? Without something to write with? He mentioned that he can't read, so there'd be no point in that anyway. I have no way of making him *see.*

Unless...

Swallowing hard, I reach for his hand, too fast, making him flinch. But he doesn't pull away as I lift it gently between us, pressing my lips to the center of his palm. As clearly as my ruined throat will allow, I whisper into his skin, words shaped more from breath than voice. *"They'll kill me."*

The sound scrapes painfully out like gravel. His fingers twitch against mine, and I repeat it, slower this time. *"They'll... kill... me."*

Hector's brows draw together, something breaking in his eyes when he pulls his hand back. "They kill all of us eventually." His words hang bitter in the air as he drags a hand through his hair squares his shoulders. "I just thought you were different. But you're still a monster, just like they say."

My heart cracks when I take a step closer, but he backs up, shaking his head.

"I *wanted* you to be different."

And with that, he turns away, hopping down into the cabin without another word.

I let him go, not because I want to—*fuck*, I don't—but because I don't know how to stop him. The weight of what I can't say festers behind my ribs as I stare at the spot where he stood, wishing he'd come back and talk to me. Look at me again like I'm not a monster.

He trusted me enough to lift him onto my shoulders, but did I just lose that trust? Did I ruin it?

I don't have an answer. Not one I can live with, anyway, so I turn back to the task at hand. Once each barrel is full, I seal them tight for delivery, keeping one for myself.

Then I strip off my clothes and step under the falls, barely flinching when the cold hits my skin. Bathing in the river is out of the question—too full of rotting bodies and waste from the prison. It's why no one crosses it, unless I take them by boat, but the waterfall is cleaner. Still tinted from the rain, but nowhere near the sludge that surrounds Zone T.

I wash the blood and sweat from my body beneath the rushing water, hunching my shoulders to ward off the shame. Frigid water burns my skin.

If only it could wash the filth from my soul, too.

Later, once the stars have begun to shine overhead, I creep down into the cabin with quiet, practiced steps. The less noise I make at night, the less chance a biter tries to test my patience by trying to climb on board.

My book waits where I stashed it, and I slip it free from my nightstand, hugging the soft leather to my chest. When I step back into the galley, intent on reading under the moonlight, movement down the hall catches my eye.

I turn to spot Hector curled on his bench, blanket half-kicked off in his sleep. One leg hangs limply over the edge, his curls a mess, plush lips parted as he breathes through his mouth.

My throat tightens at the sight. I shouldn't watch him sleep...but I do.

He's beautiful like this, completely unguarded and relaxed. A slight sound escapes him, almost like a sigh as he shifts, brows twitching like he's caught in a dream.

Stepping forward before I can stop myself, I lay the blanket gently back over his hip. My fingers pause a beat too long on the fabric, craving to touch him, even if he'll never know.

"You're still a monster, just like they say," he'd said earlier. Maybe I am.

My knees hit the floor beside the bench, and I set the book down to let my fingers hover over him. They move lower...and lower, until they touch his ankle.

He twitches in his sleep, but doesn't wake.

Trailing upward, I brush over the curve of his calf, careful of the bandage. He's warm beneath my touch, his skin soft enough to bruise. My breath catches when he shifts again, this time toward me, the blanket falling away from his chest.

His shirt rides up, exposing a sliver of stomach and the dip of his waist. I swallow hard as my cock twitches to life. With trembling hands, I push the fabric higher, baring more of him inch by inch. My fingertips trace the lines of his jutting ribs and dusky nipples until my palm settles just over his heart.

Thump. Thump. Thump.

Still beating. Still *mine.*

"Charon..." he sighs again, licking his lips.

My cock fills rapidly at the sound of my name on his tongue. Fuck, is he dreaming of me? Do I make him feel safe?

Does he want me as much as I want him?

Leaning in, I press my forehead to his sternum, letting myself breathe in his scent. He twitches a bit, but otherwise, stays asleep. I drag my lips across the bare skin just above his waistband, and when he moans softly, I answer with another kiss, this one to the hollow of his throat. My body vibrates with restraint as I fight the primal need to sink my teeth into his flesh, mark him up so that the world knows he's mine.

Carefully, I drag my fingers down again, this time not stopping at his ribs. My palm slides over his stomach, thumb grazing the faint dip of his navel, pulse hammering as I inch downward until I find the hem of his pants—

And stop myself from going further.

Hector whimpers in his sleep, hips pressing into my touch. The apparent erection tenting his crotch makes my mouth water, but I lay one more kiss on his throat before pulling away.

As lonely as I've been, as desperately as I want him, I'm not the monster he thinks I am. I'll prove it.

He'll realize soon enough that he belongs to me, anyway, and when he does, I won't need to take. He'll give himself freely, willingly. Not because I forced him, but because he knows that I belong to him, too.

And when that happens, no one will take him away. Not even death.

Gods have mercy on anyone who tries.

CHAPTER NINE

The monster's been up there for hours.

After hobbling down the stairs yesterday, I'd flopped back onto my bench, angry and still exhausted from getting shot at. Sometime in the middle of formulating a plan to get inside Zone T, I must have fallen asleep, because it was morning when I'd opened my eyes again. And Charon was still up on the deck.

I'd poked around more, examining the sorry excuse for provisions in his cabinets, which is how I found the jar full of eyeballs currently staring at me on the table. I'd nearly screamed.

My intention was to confront him about it, ambush him when he came back down and demand to know what the *fuck* he plans on doing with me, but...well, he never ended up coming back down. The scent of smoke has been drifting into the cabin all day, and now that night has long since fallen, my curiosity is getting the better of me.

I creep back onto the steps, wincing when my knee presses on a loose board, causing it to squeak. My ears prick to listen for any signs of footsteps, but all I hear is the crackle of a fire. Sterilizing water, maybe?

One peek onto the deck confirms my suspicion when I spot him sitting before some kind of fire pit, a pot boiling above the flames. His head is bent, hair tied back from his face as he concentrates on a stick in his hands, whittling away at it with a knife.

My pulse kicks up, not because of the weapon, but because he's... completely *naked*.

From his massive shoulders to the thick calves above his feet, the monster hasn't a shred of clothes on.

Heat rushes to my cheeks when my eyes run over the hair on his chest, the hard ripple of muscled biceps as he carves away at the branch, abs flexing with each movement. He's all hard lines and tanned skin, built like an oak tree, no stranger to hard labor. Probably from operating the boat. It isn't until my perusal falls on the long cock resting between his thighs that I rip my gaze up to his face—

And find him staring straight at me.

The jar of eyeballs slips from my sweaty grip, hitting the deck before rolling toward him, stopping only once it hits his foot. But he keeps his attention on me.

"I, uh..." Frozen in place, my heart roars in my ears as I try to think of something to say, all of my strength focused on keeping my gaze above his hips. Horror washes over me when I feel the tightness in my pants as my dick starts to swell.

No, no, fuck no.

Not him.

Charon tilts his head, raising a brow when he looks down at the jar resting against his toes, and I finally find the words to speak.

"I found that. In the cupboard." My voice comes out scratchy, so I clear my throat. "Do you collect those like some sort of sick freak?"

His gaze snaps up to mine, features growing cold as he sets aside the knife and stick. Reaching for the jar, he clicks his tongue three times, and a squawk answers from the trees.

Nyx flutters down onto his shoulder, talons digging into his skin, but he barely flinches. He opens the jar, holding it up to her with his gaze trained on me. The bird dives beak-first into it, where she fucking swallows an eyeball *whole*.

The monster beckons me closer, curling a finger in a way that does nothing to ease the situation between my legs.

I cross my arms with a scowl, thankful that the stairs hide the lower half of my body. "I'm coming nowhere near your murder bird when she's munching on human eyes."

Or your naked dick.

His lips twitch, but he just caps the jar and shrugs, grabbing his branch again to continue on with...whatever it is he's doing. Nyx croaks loudly before taking off back into the trees, leaving six long scratches on his shoulder. From the scars crisscrossing his skin, it seems this is a regular occurrence for them. A line of blood trickles onto his pec, rolling over a taut nipple, but he does nothing to wipe it away. Like being covered in blood comes naturally to him.

I blink rapidly for several seconds, watching the crimson drip onto his thigh, far too close to that dangling appendage I'm trying my damndest not to look at...and failing.

It's just *there*. Thick and veiny even while flaccid, nestled between his balls. Not overly humongous but still symmetrical to his body. As tan as the rest of him, like he frequently sunbathes in the nude.

Truth be told, I haven't seen many cocks. When every single day is a fight for survival or a struggle to eat, sex is the last thing on the mind, but Charon's is probably the nicest one I've laid eyes on. Very clean. Part of me wishes I could get a closer look.

He clears his throat, though, causing it to twitch, and I drop my scowl to the floor, cheeks burning. Every muscle locks up when he stands and turns around, the urge to examine his ass so strong that I squeeze my eyes shut. Clothing rustles, fabric sliding against skin. It isn't until I hear chair legs scrape on wood that I crack open a lid, finding him back in his seat with a pair of damp pants on.

The shirt he was wearing earlier hangs from the railing, dripping wet as the waterfall rushes behind him, no longer hitting the boat. He must have been washing his clothes.

A wooden ladle appears in his hands, and he stirs the pot over the fire before using the spoon to pour some of its contents into a dented thermos. The sweet berry scent fills my nostrils, making my stomach growl angrily. Charon once again meets my gaze as he offers the thermos to me, lips quirking at the corners.

I scramble onto the deck without making sure my dick is in check, because I'm too fucking thirsty to refuse. It's demoralizing, the way I crawl toward him, but hopping on one leg would probably be worse. When I'm close enough, I snatch the thermos from his grasp before gulping down the boiling liquid, not even caring when my mouth blisters with burns.

The monster gapes at me, his hand hovering in mid-air like he'd been seconds away from stopping me, but it's too late. I drain the thermos completely.

Back at Aster's Hollow, there's a belief that rotters can't feel pain, that the infected gene destroys that part of our brain. There's some truth to it, I suppose. I *can* feel pain, but it's usually fleeting. Some people feel none. Some spend their entire existence in agony. How the infection affects us is different for each individual, but we all have one singular thing in common—the possibility of turning into biters.

At some point in our lives, the infection *might* take over. It could happen tomorrow, next week, thirty years from now, or in thirty seconds. If we're lucky, maybe never. Essentially, we're all ticking time bombs, which is why everyone treats us like trash. From what I've overheard, it's why Zone T separates their rotters from the rest of the prisoners, too. The stories the soldiers have told over the years are too horrible to believe, and yet I fear they tell the truth.

That's why I need to get inside. To find my sister.

Charon doesn't speak—not that he could. Even if he did, I don't think he'd find the words to match the look on his face. He just stares at me like I grew another head as I wipe my mouth, smearing blood across my chin. My lips are raw, scalded from the liquid, but it doesn't matter. The burn is already fading, healing fast.

His gaze flicks to the thermos, then to my face. My mouth and eyes.

I hand it back to him wordlessly, a shiver running down my spine when his fingers brush mine. Curiosity lights his features, a tilt to his head that tells me he's got a question burning but can't figure out how to ask.

Fuck, how would that feel to be trapped inside your head like that? Words crawling around with no way out?

"It happened when I was nine," I mutter, throat still raw from the liquid. "My sister wanted to see Zone T's watchtowers, just once. She was...*is* older than me."

Charon doesn't blink, focusing on me intently.

"We climbed one of those maple trees to get a look above the treeline, but..." I pause, the words like gravel in my mouth. "A red storm rolled in without warning. She always carried this old tarp in her pack for emergencies. Said it made her feel like she had control, I guess? Like she could keep us safe." My voice hitches. "She threw it over the branch, tucked us underneath, and told me to stay still. But I slipped."

The Ferryman shifts closer, his body heat warming my skin.

"My foot went out, and I fell straight through the branches. Hit the ground so hard that it knocked the air from my lungs. The rain got into my mouth, my eyes. I swallowed it before I even realized what I was doing."

The sound of the branches cracking, the sudden drop, my sister's shriek echoing off the forest mist will forever haunt me. "I broke my arm, got a few scrapes, but I didn't feel anything at first. Then the fever hit. My vision started going dark, and I was *so fucking cold.*"

Charon's eyes glimmer, lips parting slightly as his fingers twitch like he wants to reach out. But he doesn't.

"I blacked out," I whisper, swallowing hard. "Usually happens when I get caught in red rain, and a frenzy takes over. Lucky for her, she was up in that tree, but all she could do was watch while her little brother lost his fucking mind. I ran off into the trees, and she stayed up there for almost two days until the weather finally cleared. Took her forever to find me, face down in the dirt, covered in blood. I...I still don't know where it came from..."

My voice falters, but I press on, letting all of this pour out of me like an open wound. "My sister didn't say anything right away. She waited until we were home, until she'd cleaned me up and tucked me in. Then she told our father." A breath rattles out of me. "He didn't take it well. Said that my eyes looked wrong and that there was something inside me now. That it was like looking at a corpse instead of his son. I think he was right."

Neither of us moves for a moment. The silence is heavy, only the rush of the waterfall and crackling flames filling the space. But then Charon leans forward slowly. His arm extends, tentatively, before he finally settles his palm on my shoulder. The warmth of it breaks something in me.

Blinking hard, I clear my throat, unsure why I'm telling this giant fucking stranger my life story. "Anyway, it was just me and Lena after that. She told me it didn't matter, and I was still me. That she'd protect me no matter what. She left for Zone T a year later after telling me that she'd discovered something big, something that could help a lot of people. Haven't seen her since. That was ten years ago." I drag a hand through my hair, suddenly self-conscious. "It doesn't matter. I'll find her. That's why I started a fight with those soldiers before they dragged me to you, I knew they'd bring me here—"

I don't realize I'm crying until Charon's other hand comes up to cradle the side of my face. His thumb brushes the tear from my cheek, and when I look at him again, there's no pity in his gaze. Just raw adoration and something like...awe. The reverence in his touch makes my whole body tremble.

Closing my eyes, I lean into his palm, allowing myself a moment of weakness. "You don't scare me, you know," I whisper, unable to watch his reaction to my confession.

A soft gasp leaves his throat before his fingertips fall away, and my lids pop open in time to see him grab out the stick that he'd been whittling. I blink in confusion as he turns it over in his hands, showing me the bend at the top, shaped like a hooked handle. There are grooves along the side where his knife carved small, steady patterns.

It takes my brain too long to understand what he's showing me, but when I do, my breath catches. He slides off his chair to kneel in front of me, holding it out with both hands, like an offering. My throat closes, almost too tight to speak.

"You..." I start, then shake my head. "You made this?"

The details are beautiful, each notch carefully measured, each groove smooth under his thumb. Reaching out slowly, my hand shakes as I take it from him before using it to stand.

It's solid and strong, the handle fitting perfectly under my armpit to lean on.

I try to speak again, but nothing comes out, my emotions frayed from baring my soul to him. So I just nod, too stunned for words, and when I finally meet his gaze, he nods too. Relief softens the harsh planes of his face.

Did he do this for me? Or maybe he just needed to keep his hands busy? Why would he help me like this? No one's ever...

Charon settles back into his seat, a soft smile playing on his mouth as he gazes toward the horizon. He crosses his arms over his bare chest, thighs widening. The irrational thought of crawling into his lap has me looking away.

"Thank you," I finally whisper, sitting back down next to the fire.

He doesn't respond other than holding out his hand, eyes still trained on the pinkening sky, and I...

I take it.

Our fingers thread together as we watch the sun rise in silence, and for the first time since I can remember—since before Lena left, before the hunger and constant fight to live—I just *exist*.

For one split second, hope sparks in my chest that maybe things will be okay.

But then thunder rolls in the distance. The clouds take on a ruddy tint as the sun rises higher, reminding me where we are. Who I'm with.

I've let my guard down, but I need to prepare myself.

This is Zone T, where prisoners go to die.

And once you board the Ferryman's boat...you're never heard from again.

Charon

They come for the water in the morning.

Sometime after dawn, Hector had fallen asleep on the deck, curled onto his side with the cane I'd made him clutched tightly to his chest.

I watch him for as long as I can, remembering the words he told me last night, still reeling from the shock of it. The fall, his father's abandonment, and his sister...Lena...

I don't even know how to process that part.

His lashes fall over his cheeks, lips parted and stained faintly with dried blood. The soft curls on his head are a mess, stuck to his forehead, half-wild from sleep. He's breathing slowly, a small crease lingering between his brows even in rest.

He doesn't know how to be still. Not really. But at this moment, he looks peaceful, like someone who hasn't spent his entire life running and starving.

It hurts to wake him.

But the Judge waits for no one.

The rumble of their engine is the first thing I hear, echoing faintly through the trees. Tires crunch over gravel from their solar-powered truck, boots stomping through brush when they approach the boat.

I touch Hector's shoulder gently. He flinches awake, immediately reaching for the cane with wide, unfocused eyes. Pressing a finger to my lips, I gesture to the water barrels before helping him up. When he's standing steady enough, I let him go to grab the pulley and lower the ramp in time for a group of soldiers to appear on the dock.

To my immediate displeasure, the one leading them is the nose-less asshole who dropped my rations so far away, the same one who shot at Hector's feet when he tried to retrieve them for us. Jonas.

Dance, rotter, dance.

My fists clench when he steps onto the boat with a harsh, ugly sneer.

"Well, looky here," he drawls, eyeing Hector with a dark look. "The freak kept you alive. Thought for sure he'd have eaten you by now."

Hector grips his cane tighter, glaring at the soldiers as they start moving barrels off the boat, but he keeps his mouth shut.

Jonas doesn't like that.

"You hear me, rotter?" He moves closer, and I stiffen when he points his rifle right at Hector's chest. "I'm talking to you."

Hector doesn't flinch at the rifle, just curls his lip in disgust as he studies the man's ruined face.

"Are you fucking deaf?" Jonas spits, lifting the gun to jab the barrel into Hector's forehead. "I said—"

Lunging forward quickly, I step between Hector and the rifle, my heart racing as I lift my palms. Hector shifts behind me, readying to swing his cane, but I throw an arm out to stop him with a harsh whisper. *"Calm."*

Jonas gazes between us, cruelty glinting in his eyes. "Oh, I see. The freak likes to *play* with his food. Must get pretty lonely out here, huh?"

Hector exhales furiously at the insinuation. I step forward again, just enough to back Jonas up onto the ramp. He's still smirking, but he takes a step off the boat, his finger leaving the trigger.

My shoulders relax slightly. But then Hector speaks.

"Watch your fucking mouth," he mutters under his breath, quiet but still audible enough to make me flinch. Jonas' smile dies.

"You got something to say, sweetheart?" he snarls, cocking the rifle with a mechanical click.

"Yeah," Hector answers, despite me shaking my head to tell him *no*. "I said watch. Your. *Fucking*. Mouth."

Jonas's eyes flash, metallic glinting in the cavern on his face as he opens his mouth, whipping the gun in Hector's direction.

I step forward fast, spreading my arms wide as a growl scrapes my throat.

Jonas barks out a laugh, shoving the barrel against my chest. "Move, freak, or I'll put so many holes in you that your rotter won't know which one to fuck."

Hector steps up beside me, the heat of his anger scalding hot. "Put one bullet in him and you'll be swallowing your own teeth, motherfucker."

I throw an arm back to hold him off, not because I doubt him, but because he's *mine* to protect. The other soldiers snicker, clearly enjoying the show.

"You rotten piece of shit." Jonas tries to get around me, but I block his view, backing us up. "Is that a threat?"

Hector peeks around my torso, baring his teeth in a fierce grin that would have made my cock hard if I weren't currently trying to save his life. "Wouldn't be the first soldier I've killed, and you sure as shit won't be the last."

That does it.

Jonas lunges, rifle swinging toward Hector, but my hand darts out to grab the barrel mid-swing. With a *crack*, I wrench it sideways and slam it across his face. He stumbles back, spurting blood as I grab his vest and pound his head into the railing hard enough to make a dent.

He crumples to the ground, rolling off the ramp onto the dock while the other soldiers back away to make room, none of them offering their assistance. Why would they? Every single one of them had been a prisoner at some point, criminals taken to Zone T until they earned their freedom in the pit.

There's no honor amongst thieves.

Jonas coughs, wheezing as he climbs to his feet. "You're dead. Worse than dead. The shit I'm gonna do to you will make you wish you were—"

A clap of thunder rolls through the clouds, echoing off the surrounding mountains.

Everyone freezes. The sky begins to darken, shifting from deep pink to a heavy, bruised red as every soldier on the dock stiffens. Jonas lowers the rifle, swollen eyes darting up toward the horizon as a sliver of lightning cracks the sky, casting his sneer in stark, blood-colored light.

"Shit," one of the soldiers hollers, panicked. "Red rain. We need to get inside."

"Guess you freaks get to live another day." Jonas spits at my feet, turning hard on his heel. "We'll be back when the rain stops, and your little fuck toy better be ashes by then."

He shouts for the others to hurry, and they scatter fast, boots pounding as they hop back into their vehicle. The engine roars to life, and they vanish into the tree line like rats before a flood.

I stay rooted in place, watching the sky churn above as dark red bleeds into black. It's been months since the infected rain last fell. There's no warning for it, no pattern. It comes when it wants and lasts as long as it pleases, soaking the ground, seeping into lungs, turning ordinary people into mindless, starving biters.

Unless you're immune, like me, or have the infected gene, like...

Spinning toward Hector, I catch sight of his pale face turned toward the clouds, lips set in a grim line. The rain affects rotters differently, amplifying their senses, cranking up their instincts to full volume. Some get violent, some go feral—snarling, biting, forgetting their own name. And some...some need to fuck.

Not want. *Need.*

Another crack of thunder rumbles around us, followed by a vein of lightning flashing directly above. Electric static raises the hair on my arms, and Nyx announces her arrival with a loud caw before landing on my shoulder.

"In we go, in we go," she croaks, feathers ruffled.

My pulse races as I study the sharp rise of Hector's chest, the way his fingers flex tighter around the cane, tension tightening his shoulders. Stormlight catches in his eyes as his pupils expand, completely swallowing the green when he swings his gaze toward mine.

"If you've got a door with a lock," he whispers, "I'd get behind it. *Now.*"

CHAPTER ELEVEN

Charon

The first drop hits the deck, splattering the wood like blood, but I don't move.

Hector's breathing has gone shallow, his grip on the cane trembling. "Please," he begs, voice cracking. "Charon, go. Lock yourself in. I can't—" He sways slightly, stumbling back a step before catching himself on the railing. "I can't control it when the rain hits."

Nyx nips at my ear before taking shelter below deck, and I rush toward him to help.

"Go!" His angry gaze snaps to mine as he tilts forward, cane dragging behind him. "I don't want to hurt you, just…please go!"

I shake my head firmly, because I'm not leaving him out here like this, not when he's breaking apart right in front of me.

He stares at me, horrified, shoulders heaving. His lips curl as he lets out a snarl, every breath ragged and uneven when he tries to brace himself against the railing, but it's no use. The rain's working its way inside, under his skin, into his blood.

His fingers tighten around the cane before he tosses it away, where it's quickly swallowed by red puddles of water. "I said, go! I can't hold it!"

His pupils blow wide, jaw clenched so tight I hear his teeth grind as one hand fists in his hair, yanking hard. I step forward to stop him from hurting himself, but he *lunges* away from me, hitting the deck as he tries to throw himself overboard.

I barely manage to catch him before he reaches the edge and he thrashes in my grip, a broken sound tearing from his throat. Holding firm, my arms wrap around his waist even as he claws at me, nails raking down my chest. Skin splits open, but I don't let go, hauling him toward the cabin.

"You're gonna get yourself killed," he cries, breath hot against my collarbone, "and it's gonna be my fault!"

I don't care.

I just tighten my grip in response, the rain soaking through both our clothes when I stumble down the steps. With one hand, I manage to get the doors shut as he collapses against me, fists still twitching like he wants to fight, but he's already unraveling, burning up from the inside.

His forehead presses against my chest as his entire body thrums with the infection, instincts screaming for violence, for anything to release the pressure inside him.

Before I can get us to my cot, Hector grabs my biceps with bruising force, a snarl ripping from his mouth as he launches upward. I move to the side, barely avoiding a bite to the neck when his teeth sink into my shoulder, white-hot pain lancing through the muscle. A garbled shout leaves my lungs when we topple over onto the floor, his teeth embedded in my flesh.

I brace my hands against his torso to fight him off, preparing for the pain of muscle separating from bone, but it never comes.

Instead, Hector straddles me, feral noises clawing out of his throat as he starts to move against me, driven by the need to rut. I go still when his crotch rubs against mine, the friction of his hard cock making mine jump. Instinctively, my hands fall to his waist, my every intention focused on keeping him still, getting him to stop, only...I don't.

My hands seem to move on their own, helping him along while I pant heavily. My own length starts to throb with need. Thrust for thrust, I meet his movements, the pleasure mixing with the pain when he bites down harder.

It's frenzied and desperate, wrong on all accounts, but I'm powerless to stop when my orgasm slams into me unexpectedly.

Wrapping an arm around his back, I hold him in place as cum floods my pants, spilling down my thigh.

Hector grinds down on me, grunting and whining while his hips continue to move like he's searching for something, *anything* to bring him what he needs.

When I finally come down, still trembling from the small spurts dripping from my cock, I realize what his body craves. *Release.*

"Shh." I try to soothe him as I reach between us, popping the buttons on his trousers. *It's okay. I know what you need. I'm going to help you.*

Snagging his waistband, I slowly drag it down, and my fingers wrap tightly around his shaft when it springs free. He snarls, but doesn't loosen his jaw, mindlessly thrusting into my fist as I give him something to rut into.

His cock is thick and heavy, slick with precum that covers my palm. He tenses against me, breathing hard, and warmth floods my hand when he starts to come. White, sticky ropes land on my abdomen as he shudders, his snarls morphing into low moans that have my spent length filling once more.

When Hector's finished, he collapses onto my chest, teeth finally letting go. Blood pours from the wound, rolling down to mix with the cum on my skin, but I don't move.

Not when he lets out a sob before curling into me, immediately latching onto my nipple before falling asleep.

I don't know what to do or what to think. Will he remember what happened when the rain stops? Will he hate me for it?

Doesn't matter. I'll deal with that later, but for now...

For now, he's safe. Out of the rain, out of Zone T and *alive*. I'll do whatever it takes to keep him that way.

Hector sleeps for hours at a time, maybe days. I lose track. The storm doesn't let up, hammering the deck above us while he clings to me through its entirety.

Sometimes he cries. Others, he wakes up long enough to bite me again and writhe into my fist before falling back asleep with his mouth latched to my nipple. I keep my cock in my pants, but I'd be lying if I said I wasn't losing myself to the pleasure every time Hector does.

All I can do is change my clothes when I can, clean the bites, and wipe away most of the blood and cum before he wakes again. Sometimes I speak to him even though I don't know what this fever-drenched version of him will remember. Don't know what he'll think when he wakes up and finds my blood under his nails or his marks on my chest.

At one point, I fall asleep myself, only to wake up to the sting of his teeth and my hands gripping his ass, helping him thrust. There's hardly time to catch my breath or drink some water before he needs me again. The bites will scar, but that thought drives me to orgasm more than his cock pulsing against my own—the idea of Hector branding me. Owning me.

Because I've claimed him.

And I want to belong to him as much as he belongs to me.

CHAPTER TWELVE

Hector

When the rain frenzy hits, I'm not in control.

It's as if all thought takes a backseat, reducing me to nothing more than an animal living off instinct to survive. Back at Aster's Hollow, they have contingencies in place for this. Bolts on doors, windows barred with whatever is available, and you'd better pray your roof doesn't leak. Everyone arms themselves: shovels, pick axes from the mine, table legs. Anything to fend off a rotter who's out of their mind.

But accidents still happen.

I was eleven when I killed for the first time.

It was shortly after Lena left, and I was alone. Starving. There hadn't been much left in the shack, so I'd ventured out to hopefully scrounge up some ration coins. I didn't get far before they found me.

Three soldiers on patrol, probably fresh out of training, drunk on power and actual liquor. All of them with silver-scarred faces. They'd laughed when they saw me, this half-dead kid in baggy clothes and muddy boots. I'd tried to run, but they were faster.

"Well, boys," one of them had snickered after taking me down, pressing my cheek into the dirt. *"Looks like we caught ourselves a stray. And do you know what happens to strays?"*

I'd fought with all the strength I had, which wasn't much. It had been days since I'd eaten anything.

The soldier had gripped my hair, pulling my head back as he straddled me from behind. *"Strays get fucked."*

They'd taken turns violating me in every way possible, only stopping when the rain began to fall. The bastards had been so distracted that they'd missed all the signs of a storm rolling in, and when the first drop hit my cheek, I froze. Felt it soak into my skin, into the cuts and bruises they'd caused with their fists.

And then I wasn't me anymore.

I don't even remember the killing. Just flashes of screaming, the taste of copper, the feel of flesh and bone giving way under my hands. When I came back to myself, I was barefoot, covered in blood, with one of their rifles clutched in my arms like a teddy bear. Their bodies were nothing but a shredded mess at my feet.

And I felt *better*. Stronger. No longer hungry or bleeding.

I didn't sleep for days after that. Every time I closed my eyes, I saw their faces and felt their hands on me. It wasn't fear that kept me awake, though; it was the shame.

They'd hurt me, so I hurt them back...and I *liked* it.

So when the frenzy hits now, when the sky turns red, I hide. I warn everyone to stay away because I know what I become.

Evil. *Rotten.*

In this world, there are no innocent people. Kill, or be killed. Eat, or be eaten. It's inevitable.

And no one is safe.

When I finally rise above the red haze in my mind, I don't know how much time has passed.

Sweat covers my skin, something solid and warm beneath me. The taste of copper pools around my lips, and when I unlatch my teeth from something soft, I go completely still.

Because there's a *breeze* blowing against my bare ass. I'm also hard, my throbbing length trapped between my body and whatever I'm lying on, the pressure causing me to give an involuntary roll of my hips.

A hitched breath brushes against my forehead.

Immediately, my eyes spring open, and the first thing I see is a pair of hooded dark blue eyes staring up at me.

Charon.

That's when I realize that I'm lying on his bare chest, *completely naked*, with my cock pressed into his abs. And there's blood on my lips. On my tongue, covering my teeth.

Lifting my head, I drop my gaze to where it all runs down his shoulder, multiple bite marks marring his flesh. One of his nipples is swollen and bruised, shiny with red-tinted spit. It's not until I register that his own hard length juts into mine from beneath his trousers that I launch off the bed, tumbling onto the floor.

"W—what the fuuuck," I stutter, scooting backward until I hit the wall, my pulse hammering loudly in my ears.

Charon sits up, raising his palms as if to calm me, but when his legs swing over the edge of the cot, my vision catches on the mess running down his torso. Streaks of red, and... and white. Dried, caked onto his skin, on *my* skin, mixing like some sick oil painting.

Blood and cum.

My gut churns as I roll onto my knees and vomit. All that comes up is stomach acid and crimson.

What did I fucking do?!

When he comes toward me, I throw my arm out to keep him back as another wave hits me, heaving so hard that my throat burns. Charon just waits, unmoving.

I spit what's left onto the floor and brace on trembling hands, unable to look at him with the proof of what I've done coating his skin.

I hurt him, just like those soldiers hurt me.

"Don't," I rasp when he moves again, my voice shredded like I've spent days screaming. "Don't come near me."

A long silence stretches out before he slowly stands, inching around me to leave. As his soft footsteps retreat, I bite my lip so hard that the skin splits.

Oh, gods, what have I done?

Collapsing to the floor, I roll into a ball as sobs wrack my body, disgusted with myself. The rain doesn't even have to touch me anymore; it's almost like the change in the atmosphere is enough to send me into a spiral. I hate it. *I hate me.* I wish I could be someone immune, like Charon. Someone the infection can't control.

Sometime later, maybe hours, I'm still rocking myself on the floor when he returns. The door creaks open, followed by the careful thud of his boots. Water splashes as he sets something down gently near my head, and I glance through my wet lashes to find a bucket, half-full of water, with steam curling off the surface and a rag inside. Next to it, he places a set of folded clothes before backing away quietly, leaving me alone again.

And fuck, somehow that makes it worse because I deserve *rage*. I deserve disgust and retaliation, not...whatever this is, especially from the man whose blood I just licked off my teeth.

I stare at the bucket for a long moment before dragging myself toward it, the mangled skin of my missing foot now healed thanks to the rain.

Charon heated the water. Probably so that I can clean the vomit from the floor.

My stomach curdles, shame gnawing deeper than the infection as I grab the rag and wring it out so that I can start to scrub. And scrub.

I don't even hear him come back.

One second, I'm trembling, trying to get the wood clean, sobbing as I desperately try to erase the stain of what I've done, to make it look like it did before I ever *ruined it*—

And the next, he's kneeling beside me, reaching for the bucket.

I flinch back, keeping my burning eyes down as I try my best to cover my nakedness. Not that it matters. "I can do it. I'll make it clean."

Not dirty. Not *rotten.*

Charon makes a noise before he dips another rag into the water. Just when I think he's going to help me scrub the floor, he lifts his hand, and...

Softly presses the cloth to my cheek.

I freeze, my gaze flying to his face as he watches me carefully. He's in a fresh shirt, long hair tied back, no trace of my shame left on his body. We stare at each other while he wipes the cloth in careful circles, washing away the dried blood on my lips and chin.

He doesn't even pause when he reaches my throat, rewetting the cloth before scrubbing me gently. Doesn't flinch at the cum flaking on my chest, in my belly button.

He just...keeps going. Patiently. No ounce of anger or hatred in his features. If anything, he looks fucking *peaceful.*

My jaw clenches so tight it hurts. "Why are you doing this?"

He doesn't answer. I mean, not that he *could.* But he doesn't respond in any way, just rinses the cloth again and wipes down my arms, my hands, the blood on my knuckles, and under my fingernails from where I must have scratched him.

By the time he reaches my flaccid dick, I'm shaking too hard to speak. He holds my gaze, cleaning me gently. The wretched thing gives a pitiful twitch at the contact but remains limp, though sensitive. Aching. As if I spent hours or even days with an erection.

That thought has me sucking in a ragged breath.

"How long?" I ask, not fully forming the question. Charon seems to understand what I want to know, anyway.

He sits back on his haunches, tossing the rag into the bucket as he looks away. When he meets my gaze again, there's a worried pinch to his brow, and he holds up four fingers.

I swallow hard, starting to shake all over again. "Hours?"

Please, be hours. Please.

His lips thin as he shakes his head slowly. *No.*

"Days?!" My fingers curl into my hair as my lungs constrict, and I bend over, bile rising in my throat once again.

Four days. I spent four fucking days in a frenzy, doing who knows what to him, over and over and *over*. A violent shudder wracks my body, the edges of my vision going white.

Four days.

What the fuck happened? *Oh, gods, will he kill me now?* I deserve to die.

Charon grabs my wrists, gently prying them from my roots before placing my hands on his chest. His skin is warm beneath my palms as I fist his shirt to keep from falling over. My throat tightens with another wave of nausea, but I swallow it back, focusing on the beat of his heart beneath my touch. No words come out when I try to speak, only a broken sound—broken like me.

Tender fingers find my jaw, raising my face, but I squeeze my eyes shut. I can't fucking look at him, even as he gently scrubs my scalp.

When was the last time someone touched me like this? Gently, almost reverently, as if I'm something close to human? Something worth taking care of? Why would he do this after what I've done?

He backs up, causing my hands to fall away, and a moment later, something soft covers my face. I open my lids to find him easing a shirt over my head as if I might shatter. My arms hang useless at my sides as he pulls the sleeves down one at a time, fingertips brushing my skin.

And I let him, because I don't remember the last time someone dressed me. Not since I was a kid, when I was too young to take care of myself.

Not since Lena.

The shirt is oversized, warm from his hands as it settles on my thighs, covering my shame. It smells like the boat—like wood and salt and *him*.

I'm still shaking.

But when he pulls me in, guiding my forehead to his shoulder, I don't pull away. Not even when he smooths a hand down my back, making me shiver.

"I'm sorry," I whisper, my voice cracking on another sob.

He just holds me tighter, pressing his lips to my curls with a contented sigh.

I know he can't speak.

But somehow, what he just did for me speaks louder than words ever could.

CHAPTER THIRTEEN

Hector

Charon stands near the window in the bathroom, the knife in his hand gliding down his cheek in slow, practiced strokes. He works without a mirror, just a faint reflection in the glass, his hair running down his back like a dark waterfall.

It shouldn't be mesmerizing, watching him shave, but my eyes keep tracking the drag of the blade, silver catching against the hollow of his throat. Who taught him to do it? A father, maybe? Brother? Some moment in his life where letting someone that close with a sharp weapon wasn't so dangerous.

"Pretty eyes," Nyx squawks from her perch above, rustling her feathers in the quiet.

The knife pauses just under his jaw before he wipes it clean, then switches sides, pulling his skin taut with one hand while the other works the edge upward. His eyes flick to mine, catching my gaze from where I sit at the kitchen table, and I drop it down to the worn wood while my pulse quickens.

How old is this boat, anyway? Where did it come from? How did he end up here? So many questions swirl around my head, but I'm too much of a coward to speak after the way he cleaned my naked body this morning.

After what I did to him.

Before me sits a tin plate with three narrow strips of dried meat on it. That's it. No bread, no broth or vegetables. Just brittle pieces of what looks like venison, maybe rabbit. I don't actually know what meat they raise inside Zone T, but whatever it is, it's all Charon has left. And he offered it to me.

I haven't touched it.

When he finishes shaving, his fingers run along his jawline, searching for anything missed stubble. My attention once again drifts back to him, to the broad cut of his shoulders and veins running down his arms. The steadiness of his hands. Part of me wonders what happened between us over the last four days. Did...did I touch him? Make him feel good? Did he touch *me?*

Charon meets my gaze once again and gestures toward the chair in the corner with a tilt of his head, knife held loosely in his grip. When all I do is stare at him, he points to his clean face, then mine, causing me to touch the hair growing wild on my cheeks. Realization dawns on me that he wants to help me shave.

I should be saying *"fuck no"* and getting far away from that blade as possible. Yet, my legs move without thought.

"Yeah, okay." Gripping the cane he made for me, I limp over quietly and take a seat.

He steps in close, the homemade soap he'd just used filling my nostrils as his palm brackets my jaw, rubbing the lather into my skin. Once finished, his fingers turn my head until the edge of the blade kisses my throat.

I should be terrified, but...I'm not. If anything, my dick twitches pathetically at the feel of his touch on my flesh. His eyes meet mine, thumb brushing over the hammering pulse point I'm sure he can feel before slowly dragging the knife down.

That first scrape of steel down my cheek is gentle but just loud enough that I can hear it over the wind outside. My breath fills the space between us, close enough that his chest brushes my shoulder when he leans in. His gaze never leaves the path of the blade.

"Why are you doing this?" I whisper when he pauses to wipe off some hair with a rag. "Why are you taking care of me?"

Something unreadable passes over his expression before he dips the knife again, thumb pressing just under my chin. It forces me to look at him while the steel glides down my neck.

There's danger in the way he holds me, but...there's also trust. Mine or his, I can't tell anymore, but the tender way he touches me even with a knife at my jugular is messing with my head. Anyone else in this position would carve me up, no hesitation

So why isn't he?

Charon's eyes linger at my mouth when he leans in for the final stroke. His knuckles brush my lips, and my heart pounds against the knife's edge, all of my blood surging toward my cock as I exhale.

He swallows hard, pulling back now that he's finished, and I drop my gaze down to the very apparent bulge between his legs, feeling...I don't even know how I feel.

Fuck, I think I might like the Ferryman more than I should. It's terrifying.

"You should eat," I croak to distract myself from his erection, gesturing toward the meat on the table.

He just shrugs, tapping the counter thrice with his knuckles in a non-answer, but I feel like I can hear his response perfectly. *So should you.*

My jaw tightens. "You don't have to give me your food. I'll be okay."

Another shrug. Gods, he's so damn stubborn, and I hate that a part of me...likes it.

Silence stretches on until I finally give in, hobbling over to the table to bite into the smallest strip. It's tough, salty, and clings to my teeth like leather, but I force it down. The meat settles heavily in my stomach, though the guilt in my gut is heavier. I glance at the plate again with only two pieces left now. It's all we have.

"This isn't sustainable," I mutter. "We'll starve before the week's out."

Charon just sits down across from me and nods slowly, lips pressed into a grim line. I look at him—*really* look at him, studying his face. There's exhaustion in the lines of his mouth, eye sockets sunken in. Beneath the open top button of his shirt, I can see his collarbones, more prominent than they were when I first woke up on this boat.

A choked noise leaves my throat as I realize what's happening here.

He's not just keeping me alive, he's killing himself in order to do it.

Shoving the plate away, I push onto my good leg, appetite gone. "I need to get into the prison. We need supplies and I need to find my sister."

His head snaps toward me, brows raised in alarm as he wags his head back and forth.

"I know," I say quickly, holding up a hand. "I know it's basically a death sentence, but if we don't get food, we'll die anyway."

He stares at me for a long beat before rising from the bench. I watch him step up to the empty pantry, peering inside like something might magically materialize out of thin air. When he drags out the jar of eye snacks for his bird, an idea suddenly takes root in my head like the rot running through my veins.

I don't say it right away, because even *thinking* it feels insane, but desperation does funny things to a person, especially when they're starving.

I shift on my foot, swinging my gaze up to Nyx perched on the overhead beam. She tilts her head like she already knows what I'm thinking.

"What if..." I start, hesitating when Charon glances up. "What if we let her take one of my eyes?"

He goes absolutely still, hand halfway in the jar, and I grimace. Yes, if it came down to it, I'd eat the eyeballs, but I'd rather not. "She can tell who's infected, right? If she takes it from me, they might let me inside. They trust that shit."

Charon's jaw ticks as he raises his gaze to Nyx, then back to me before setting down the jar with a loud *thunk* that makes me flinch. Stepping closer, he takes my head between his palms, fingers curling into my hair as he raises my face to his with a rough shake of his head.

No.

"It's just an eye, Charon. I'm already missing a foot, I've lived through worse—"

A thumb brushes just under my right lid softly, his gaze locked desperately on mine like he's trying to memorize every color there, and my chest tightens painfully. He doesn't want me to lose my eyes because he *likes* them.

I grab both his wrists and smile sadly, knowing there's no other choice. "I can't let you die for me. Getting into Zone T is the only way."

He shakes his head again, desperately.

"Charon, *look at us*. We're out of food. You've got nothing left. You gave me everything, and what did you get in return for your troubles? Four days of assault from a half-dead rotter who can't even limp straight."

His face crumples like I've stabbed him, and I hate myself for that, but I need to make him understand.

He yanks one hand free and holds it to his pec before placing it flat against my chest. Over and over, right above our hearts, mouthing, "*mine.*"

"You're out of your fucking mind," I marvel, sucking in an exasperated breath.

He just shrugs with a nod. *Maybe I am.*

But his fingers curl around my own, thumb brushing my knuckles as he brings my palm to his lips to whisper, "*Not your eye.*"

"I'll come back. I promise. Charon, I need to do this."

He just huffs, gazing at me in frustration. After a moment, he pulls away and disappears into the bathroom. Something scrapes against the wood of the boat as he pushes out a barrel of water from the waterfall, his eyes meeting mine when he points inside it.

I grab my cane before limping over, the floor swaying underfoot as I peer into the dark depths. "What am I supposed to be looking at?"

Reaching out to touch my shoulders, he mimics the act of picking me up and setting me down inside the barrel, then does it again.

At first, I don't get it. I just stare into the water at a loss until I measure the size of it with my eyes. It's big and wide, standing as tall as my chest...big enough to fit a *person.*

"No," I breathe, stomach sinking. "You want me to get *inside* that thing?"

Charon just nods.

"No fucking way. *That's* your plan? Let them load me onto one of their vehicles like a piece of cargo and hope no one checks inside?"

All he does is point to me, then to the barrel. Then Nyx up above, like that's supposed to make this plan less terrifying.

Now that it's out there, though...I can't think of a better one.

They probably won't scan the barrels, not if he's been filling them for years. Especially if Nyx is circling like always, giving them a clear *good to go.* Still...

I drag a hand down my face, blowing out a harsh breath. "What if I can't get back out?"

He tilts his head as I look at the barrel again, dread crawling up my spine. It's tight, wet, and dark. No air holes. No guarantee I'll make it to the other side.

But it's a way in. It's a chance I'm willing to risk it all to take. Staying here means starvation for both of us.

So I square my shoulders, pulse thudding behind my ribs as I nod slowly. "Okay. Let's try it, then. See if I fit."

Charon holds my gaze for a long moment before moving to lift me in. I steady my breath and let him, trying not to think about the darkness inside of it and instead remembering why I'm doing this.

For him. And for *her*. Lena, my sister.

They've both done so much already. No matter what happens to me, I need to save them both.

By any means necessary.

CHAPTER FOURTEEN

Charon

Icy spray from the waterfall leaves a chill on my skin against the cold night air.

Hector sits on the edge of the deck quietly, cane resting beside him, shoulders hunched. He hasn't spoken since I woke him up on his bench earlier, dark circles prominent beneath those emerald eyes he was so eager to lose. Neither of us slept much, both tossing and turning most of the day. I fought the urge to scoop him up, bring him to my bed, and never let him go.

What happened between us was influenced by red rain, I know that, and yet, after four days of him using me however he needed, I feel even more protective of him. My every instinct screams to keep him close, keep him *alive*.

But I've always struggled with protecting those I care for, so instead, I focus on the rhythm of my work. Drag a barrel across slick wood, fill it beneath the fall, let the water thunder in until the slosh grows heavy. Then I roll it to the far side of the boat to join the others.

Slowly, I ready them all, except for the one he'll hide in. That barrel, I leave for last.

When I look up, Hector is watching me closely, fists clenched tight in the folds of his sweater. He doesn't flinch when I meet his gaze, and I wish with all my heart that he'd tell me to stop. Say that it's too dangerous, that he changed his mind.

But all he does is stare. How I yearn to ask what he's thinking beneath those soft curls.

Once the barrel is half full, I peel off my shirt and beckon him closer. He hesitates only a moment before grabbing his cane, limping toward me with guarded features. Each step he takes fills me with dread, the thought of putting him in danger almost more than I can stand.

The water's chill soaks into my pants as I kneel down, and when he finally stops in front of me, I tug at the hem of his sweater tentatively.

Hector's eyes widen a fraction, breath catching, but he doesn't stop me from lifting it slowly over his head. I toss the soaked fabric aside, revealing pale skin stretched thin over bruises and sharp, bony features. Far too thin, way too fragile.

My gaze lingers on his nipples before dropping down to a jagged scar across his side, and my fingers brush over the raised flesh as I furrow my brows questioningly. *How?*

His delicate throat flexes with a swallow. "Soldiers attacked me when I was eleven. I beat them to death...but not before they carved a piece of me out first."

My heart lurches at the thought of him needing to defend himself so young, how scared and alone he must have been. Where were his parents? Why wasn't anyone around to save him?

Yet here I am, sending him to his possible death inside a prison far worse than all of his darkest nightmares. How am I any different than his sister for leaving him behind? The thought of being like her makes me sick.

Touching the scar lightly, I lower my head and gently press my lips to it.

He shudders as he drops the cane, hands falling to my shoulders. I let my mouth linger there, memorizing the shape of his hurt, honoring the place he bled and survived. Then I trace his flesh with my tongue, moving up from his sternum to his nipples before stopping at the heart beating wildly in his chest. When I finally lift my head, his green eyes are dazed, jaw hanging slack.

"You don't have to do this," I wish I could say. *"You've already survived enough."*

But I can't.

So instead, I stand and cup the back of his neck, my thumb brushing the hollow behind his ear as I touch my forehead to his. Our noses brush, breaths mingling. A choked noise claws its way out of Hector's throat when his grip on me tightens, and he leans up on his toes to press his mouth to mine.

The kiss is shaky, but there's nothing hesitant about the way he melts for me. I kiss him back with everything I can't say, our tongues dancing to some unknown yet familiar rhythm as I pull our bodies flush.

As soon as his chest meets mine, though, he jerks back so forcefully that he would have fallen had I not been holding him up.

"Fuck." His swollen lips part as he drops his dilated pupils down to his crotch—to the bulge tenting his pants. Sucking in a sharp breath, he twists around on one foot, hands moving to shield himself from my gaze in shame.

My heart aches, but I don't let go.

Instead, I step in close enough that his back warms my front. When my hands slide over his chest, brushing over his nipples, he lets out a sob.

"Hector," I whisper without sound, letting his name live inside my soul.

He goes absolutely still, and I lean forward to nip his ear as my own hard cock rests against his ass.

Don't hide from me. Please.

Pressing my lips to the side of his throat, I let him feel my acceptance in the softness of my kiss. His entire body shivers, but this time, he doesn't pull away. The trembling slows when my mouth drifts lower, skimming along the curve of his spine. I trace the edge of his shoulder blade with my tongue, taste the salt on his skin, feel the goosebumps bloom beneath my touch. And still, he doesn't stop me.

His hands clench at his sides, but when I reach around to grip his length, he gasps and grabs my wrist, moving my palm up and down. I cup his jaw just enough to see the anxiety there, but I kiss it away, swallowing every noise he makes.

He feels so good in my arms, and it's been so long since I've touched anyone this way, ten years spent alone on this boat with only Nyx and the soldiers forcing me to take them across the river. Most people are cruel or terrified of me.

Hector used to be terrified. But he's not anymore.

I lower us down to the deck carefully, laying his body beneath mine. Curls stick to his forehead, chest heaving, but he spreads his legs for me. When I settle between them, pressing our bodies together, he arches up instinctively with a desperate sound that goes straight to my bones.

"Charon," he breathes, voice ragged.

I answer with a searing kiss as his hands roam my back, fingertips dragging through water still clinging to my skin. His hips rock up against me greedily, and I sigh into his mouth, grinding my cock against him.

My lips trail over his jaw, his throat, down to his collarbone, where his pulse thrums wildly against my tongue. As I sink my teeth in, he arches again, grabbing the back of my head to keep me in place.

"Oh, gods, that feels...harder. Please."

I almost come at his mumbled plea, biting down more forcefully to suck a bruise into his flesh. He slips a hand beneath the waistband of his trousers to stroke himself as I lick away the sting of the bite. Then I do it again, and again, until his delicate throat blooms with my marks.

A collar to show the world who he belongs to.

"Help me," Hector groans, tugging down the hem of his pants. I assist him along, trailing my lips down his chest as I slide them below his hips. When his cock springs free, flushed and beautiful, I pause at his naval to look up into his heated gaze.

"Okay?" I mouth, palming my own aching length.

He nods slowly, licking his lips. "Yes. Touch me."

Those two words break something open inside my heart.

Part of me wonders if anyone has touched him this way before, but another part doesn't care, because he's here *now*. Death may wait for us tomorrow, but at this moment, he's writhing in pleasure beneath me and it's all I can offer.

Starting slow, I lightly lick around his swollen tip. Bitter salt bursts on my tongue, and Hector whimpers as his fingers tangle into my hair.

"Fuck," he hisses, hips stuttering upward.

I steady him with my hands on his thighs, thumbs tracing lazy circles when I take him deeper, his cock hot and pulsing against my tongue. With a deep moan, he throws his head back, neck arched, mouth parted in wordless surrender. His lashes flutter against flushed cheeks, curls plastered to his forehead, and the image sears itself into my memory. He's so beautiful that I have to look away, focusing on running my tongue up his length instead.

"I..." he starts, voice hoarse. "I'm close."

Tugging on my hair, he pulls me off with a soft *pop,* and I crawl up his trembling frame to kiss a trail from stomach to throat. All it takes is three more strokes before his whole body bows off the ground with a strangled cry, thick ropes of cum shooting onto his chest. I hold him through it, kissing his jaw, his temple, whispering nothing and everything all at once.

By the time his orgasm ends, he's a boneless tangle in my arms. I shift us gently, tucking him against my chest before curling my arms around him, holding tight. My own cock strains uncomfortably against my trousers, but I ignore it, content to feel Hector relax for the first time since the soldiers dragged him onto my boat.

I hate what they've done to him, then and now. What they've done to *us*. I wish I could've spared him from all of it—that scar, the pain, the weight he carries even in sleep. But I can't change the past.

All I can do is hold him now, let his breath warm my chest, and promise without words that I'm here if he needs me. He doesn't have to face the world alone anymore.

Even if he leaves when this is all over, when he finds his sister and they head out for a better life, I'll remember this forever.

In a world built to ruin people like us, moments like these are too few. Not once in all my life have I ever felt something like this. Like *him*.

So I'll cling to it for as long as I can.

CHAPTER FIFTEEN

Hector

Charon's mouth should be declared a dangerous weapon. I think I'm still seeing stars.

The deck is cold against my back, but his body keeps me warm as he reads that old book like he didn't just ruin me with his tongue. My pants are still halfway down my legs while the river sways gently around us, uncaring of how my cock lies satisfied against my thigh.

Even after falling asleep, I still feel like I'm floating high above the clouds.

These last few hours play on a loop behind my eyes—the delicate way in which he took me apart. No one has treated me so tenderly before. Like a *person*, not just another rotter who could turn at any moment. I don't know how to process it all, so I focus on the Ferryman instead.

Rolling to my side, I watch Charon read in fascination, studying the way his lips move silently as he skims the page. Every now and then, his brows furrow, deep in thought.

"Where did it come from?" I murmur, nestling into his shoulder. "The book, I mean."

He pauses, then taps the cover gently before pressing his palm to his chest. *Mine.*

"No shit. But where did you get it? I thought all the books were gone."

His finger juts upward toward the sky after pointing to his stomach.

From above. Eat?

I frown, trying to piece together what he's telling me. "You...found it inside Nyx's belly?"

Shaking his head with a snort, he flips to the inside cover and trails a finger over the faded writing scrawled in the corner. There's a lightness to his touch, like he's afraid the letters might rub away if he presses too hard.

When I still stare in confusion, he catches my hand and pulls it to his lips, mouthing a single word against my palm, *"Mother."*

"Oh," I whisper, chest tightening. "She gave it to you."

Charon smiles sadly, blue eyes swinging toward the horizon, lost in memory.

"What...what happened to her?"

His smile falters, grip tightening on mine. For a moment, I think he won't answer, but then he looks down, curling his fingers inward towards his ribs—his *heart*—before dragging them upward and out like a bird fluttering away.

Gone.

My throat swells at the desolation on his face. "She died?"

He hesitates, then nods, pointing toward Zone T in the distance.

The prison. *His mother died inside the prison.*

So many questions run through my head, like how did it happen? Is that where he grew up? Why was his mother there? Asking feels like hurting him, though, and knowing the answers won't change anything for either of us.

Maybe some things are better left in the past.

I shift closer, looping my arm through his as I rest my head on his shoulder. "I'm sorry. Mine died, too, after birthing me. Father left when I was little, and Lena...well. You know that story."

He doesn't respond. At least, not out loud, but the way he leans into me with the book still cradled between us says enough. Something tells me she's the reason he is who he is.

Soft. Gentle. Far too kind for a world so cruel.

The pages rustle in the breeze, and even if I never get to know her name, I swear I'll honor his mother for loving him every time he reads them beside me.

A sharp flutter and a scratch of talons pulls my eyes to the railing, where Nyx lands in a messy sweep of black feathers. She shakes herself once, then lets out a throaty, *"pretty eyes. Fail, fail."*

"Who taught her to speak, anyway?" I murmur, watching the murder bird as she watches me back.

Charon quirks his lips at her before tapping his chest. *Me.*

My brows jump in surprise. "You did? How is that possible?"

His eyes darken, shadows gathering in the blue, and he looks back to his book with a shrug, leaning against me.

I don't press him, even though I desperately wish I could. Maybe some things aren't meant to be explained, or maybe he physically *can't*.

Maybe one day...if we survive at all, maybe he can teach me to read that book of his, so that I can learn to know him better. I think I desperately want that.

My arm stays entwined with his as he reads into the night, Nyx's dark silhouette still perched above us, carrying a piece of him I'll never fully understand.

Morning rises far too quickly, waterfall mist soaking my clothes.

Charon stands behind me as I stare into the half-filled barrel, dark water sloshing against the sides. I know he's waiting for me to give the go-ahead, and I know we're running out of time, but...I'm slightly terrified.

The barrel looks tight and cold. Suffocating. Once the lid is on, there will be no air. I suppose with the rotter genes, I could probably hold my breath longer than a normal human, but I've never tested it before. What if I end up dying inside this thing?

But we have no other choice.

"I'm ready," I murmur, bracing my hands on the lip. "Lift me in."

There's a beat of silence before I feel him step closer, large hands curling around my waist. My pulse kicks up at his touch. He lifts me slowly, arms steady despite my weight, and the chill from the water punches up my spine as he lowers me in. I gasp, clenching my jaw when the icy liquid hits my thighs.

Charon freezes, his grip tightening ever so slightly, and I feel him lean in just enough for his breath to ghost over my ear in silent apology.

"It's fine," I grit, shaking my head. "Just...do it."

Once the water submerges my waist, he doesn't move to place the lid on. Just looks at me with a question in his eyes, one hand resting over the rim, the other finding mine beneath the surface.

Are you sure?

"I'll come back," I say again, though I'm not sure which one of us I'm trying to convince.

His lips tighten grimly, but he nods and squeezes my hand before pulling away. When I crouch down, the lid comes on, but not fully. Not until he guides us back to Zone T, where the soldiers are waiting.

He moves away, steady footsteps thumping across the deck, and then the boat begins to move. I brace myself, ducking low, elbows against the sides of the barrel as the water splashes around me. Every breath feels like borrowed time.

It doesn't take us long.

Somewhere above, Nyx caws once as the boat slows, wood creaking beneath me. My heart tries to claw its way out of my throat as Charon returns, the air shifting with his proximity even though I can't see him. He knocks softly against the barrel in a faint goodbye, and then darkness surrounds me.

The lid settles into place with a hollow finality, shutting every-thing out. No light, no oxygen, no escape. Only the slosh of water and the sound of my own heartbeat pounding in my skull.

All I can do is hope that when I see the light again, it'll be inside the walls of Zone T and not my soul crossing over to the other side.

CHAPTER SIXTEEN

Charon

The sun burns dully behind a veil of ash-stained clouds as the soldiers stomp onto the dock. Their boots hit the planks with a practiced rhythm, and I force myself to stay still beside Hector's barrel with Nyx on my shoulder.

Jonas steps onto the boat first, rifle already pointed straight at me. His mutilated face twists as he spits out a wad of something dark onto my deck before grinning.

"Morning, freak," he sneers, squinting around the boat. "That rotter of yours still hangin' round?"

I don't react as I stare him down. My muscles tense when I remember him shooting at Hector the night we'd tried to get the ration bag, and a violent urge to rip his head from his body almost consumes me.

He turns to the others, jerking his chin toward the cabin. "Search it."

They move at once, four soldiers storming aboard without hesitation, guns drawn. My pulse roars in my ears as I stay rooted to the deck, pretending I'm unbothered, even as my rage builds with every footfall.

They tear through the galley first, slamming cupboards and rattling dishes. Then the crew quarters, my cot. The closet where I kept Hector's old, bloodied clothes. One of them lingers a little too long at his bench, and I almost step forward before Rita's voice rings out sharply from the dock.

"Jonas! You wanna explain why we're wasting time ransacking our hauler when we've got deliveries?"

He scowls at me, chewing on something rancid. "This fucker's hiding something."

She just snorts in response. "You say that every time we come down here."

A moment later, the soldiers reappear, shoving past each other as they pile out. One of them shrugs. "Nothing, boss. Just a lot of dust and a jar of eyeballs. Sick fuck."

Nyx clicks her beak, feathers ruffled, and I clench my jaw as Jonas narrows his eyes but says nothing.

Rita waves a clipboard around impatiently. "Load 'em up, and be quick."

One by one, the soldiers hoist the barrels off the boat and toss them carelessly into the back of a truck. Each impact jars my spine, but I keep my face impassive, at least until they reach the last barrel.

Jonas is the one who assists in lifting it, of course. He grunts, muscles straining a little harder than usual under the weight. "Shit, this one's heavy. What the hell did you put in here, freak? Rocks?"

He doesn't wait for an answer, though, just helps drag it down the dock and shoves it into the truck with a curse before jumping into the passenger seat.

I blow out a breath, trying not to fall apart as the tailgate slams shut with a metallic *clang*. The sound reverberates through my bones. When the truck pulls away, I almost run after it, fear constricting my chest. As soon as the vehicle disappears beyond the curve of the hill, taking the most precious thing I've ever known with it, I sag against the railing in defeat.

He's gone. I'm once again alone.

But then the dock creaks behind me, and I jerk around as another group of soldiers begins bringing bags onto the boat...*ration* bags. Bulging canvas sacks of food and medicine marked with red tape.

No.

Rita leads the team. "Alright, let's get this shit on board. We got a double load today, the Judge wants a show of generosity. Aster's Hollow first, then maybe Iron Gate if we've got enough." She pauses, tossing me a wink as the morning sun sets her silver-plated skull ablaze. "Don't worry, Ferryman. We'll top off your supplies, too."

All of the blood drains from my body as realization slams into me.

Fuck.

Every few weeks or so, Zone T trades with the surrounding outposts via *my boat.* It's always sporadic, whenever the Judge sees fit. They won't even look at the water barrels until they finish—if Hector makes it that long. If he survives the ride, the heat, *the sealed lid.*

He's strong, I know he is, but that water was cold. The air was thin. What if they leave the barrels sitting in the sun too long? What if they unload everything except his and forget it on the truck bed? What if he suffocates?

Nyx gives me a disgruntled squawk, nipping my jaw before eyeing the horizon.

"*Gone,*" she croaks. "*Gone, gone.*"

I clench my fist and press it to my mouth, teeth digging into skin to keep from screaming when my eyes fall to his cane still on the ground.

He trusted me. He *trusted me.* It was all for nothing.

Once again, I'm left helpless while someone I love is hauled off to die

And just like last time... there's no one to blame but myself.

Date/Location: November 2025, Zone T
Personnel: REDACTED
Subject: ALL HOPE IS LOST

I've barricaded the south wing and
redistributed weapons to what's left of
my squad, but the inmates have taken
control.

We are no longer running a prison. We
are feeding it.

If this report ever finds its way beyond
the river, burn this place to the
ground. Salt the earth. Never come back.

Zone T is lost. It isn't a prison now.
It's something so much worse.

PART TWO

CHAPTER SEVENTEEN

Hector

My lungs are on fire.

Water laps at my chin every time the truck hits a bump, cold enough to sting the cracked skin on my lips. I can't move, arms locked tight around myself. Can't sit, can't see. Nothing to do but stand here and wait, fear consuming me the longer I'm trapped.

I try to focus on the rhythm of the truck: *one-two, one-two,* the sway of the wheels. But my thoughts crawl in like insects, buzzing, gnawing, swarming me with doubts I can't swat away.

What if I turn in here? Kill whoever opens the barrel, change them too, and unleash chaos onto the unsuspecting prison? Every soldier deserves it. The Judge, too. But most of the prisoners don't. Half of them are in here for petty crimes, like mouthing off to the soldiers or not producing enough silver. Everyone in Aster's Hollow must work in the mines in order to eat.

No silver means no ration tokens, and no tokens means no food.

A muscle spasm strikes my leg, drawing me from my thoughts, but there's no room to stretch. I grit my teeth and ride it out, counting seconds between every exhale.

Thirty-two, thirty-three...

The water's warmed slightly now, probably from my body heat. Or maybe I'm just going numb. Either way, the cold is no longer the worst part of it. Just the silence and my own ragged breathing in this wooden coffin with no guarantee I'll ever get out.

I keep seeing Charon's face, the way he looked at me last night as if I were more than just a potential threat. His warm, blue eyes and the emotions on his face were louder than what his tongue could possibly convey as he kissed me. The memory burns brighter than the pain in my lungs. I wish he were here with me right now.

The rhythm suddenly shifts as the truck begins to slow before coming to a complete stop. Pressure changes, causing the water to tilt backward and slosh into my nose, choking me. Muffled voices reach my ears, along with the hiss of brakes and gears grinding. Something bumps against the side of the barrel, making my heart leap into my throat. Then another, and another. They're unloading.

Please, let them be too lazy to notice the one with my body hiding inside.

Charon's face pops into my head again, that tight, reluctant nod right before he sealed me in. The way his hand lingered on mine like he couldn't let me go. It hits me at this moment that I don't want to leave him out there all alone, wondering what happened to me. I want to see him again, feel his forehead on mine. Return the gift he'd given me last night. *I don't want to die here.*

Another thump jostles me, pitching the barrel sideways before I can even take a breath. Water covers my body completely as I bounce off the walls forcefully. Someone's *rolling* me off the truck.

Panic floods my senses, limbs rigid as I try to catch a breath every time the water recedes from my mouth, but it's no use; the oxygen is gone.

But it's *working.* They're taking me off the truck. Holy shit, Charon's plan is working.

My heart soars at the thought of getting inside, of finding my sister and getting food, seeing her face again—

"Wait!" a familiar voice snaps harshly. Too close. "Bring that one over here."

The barrel jerks violently to a stop as I nearly bite through my tongue. *I know that fucking voice.*

My pulse thunders in my ears when heavy boots stomp closer. I can already picture that cavernous hole where his nose used to be, now filled with silver, the way he stared at me like he wanted to skin me alive. My fingers twitch in the water, itching for a weapon that isn't there, wishing I'd brought my cane with me as my head knocks against the wall when someone pushes the barrel upright.

Please. Don't open it. Don't—

CRACK.

Light explodes across my vision as the lid disappears, and for one suspended heartbeat, I meet his cold, heartless eyes.

Jonas grins wide.

"Well, well," he breathes, pointing his rifle at me. "I knew that freak was hiding something."

I lunge at him without thinking, fingers bent to claw at his face, but my body's too slow. He jerks back before I can connect, and the barrel tips over, spilling me out onto cold cement in some industrial-looking building.

"Grab him!"

More water splashes into my nostrils when I roll onto my back in time to see the butt of a gun coming toward my face.

Pain explodes briefly across my brow, fading quickly, but the hit was enough to darken my vision. I blink blearily at the odd flickering lights above—long, buzzing strips of artificial daylight that burn my eyes. A heavy boot presses against my ribs, pinning me down hard enough to restrict air as rough hands press my shoulders and legs into the floor.

Jonas stands over me, lips curled over his teeth. "Filthy fucking animal. Pretty sure the Ferryman just signed his own death warrant. The Judge won't like this."

"No, he wasn't—" I try to lift my head, opening my mouth to tell them that Charon had nothing to do with this, but another boot connects with my temple.

"Shut the fuck up, rotter!"

Fractured light bursts behind my eyes as the world tilts sideways, the ache more intense than last time. Blood drips into my eyes, obstructing my vision. Distantly, I swear I hear Nyx caw, but maybe that's just my brain bouncing around from the blow.

"What do we do with this thing, boss?" a soldier asks, holding my legs down while eyeing me in disgust.

I try to kick out with a snarl, but she grips tight, arms thicker than my torso.

Jonas leans down and rests an elbow on his knee, pressing into me harder. I wheeze but keep my glare locked on his face, refusing to look away. His eyes drag lazily over my body, searching, cataloging for weaknesses. When his gaze snags on my neck, a sneer twists his ugly face.

"What's this?" he murmurs, fingers brushing the skin beneath my jaw with a mock softness that has me flinching away. "Love bites, eh? Ain't that sweet. Lookie here, grunts, the freak's got himself a boyfriend."

One of the men snorts. "Figures. Rotters are only good for fucking."

"Fuck you," I snarl, jerking against their grip. "Let me go or I'll rip your fucking throat out with my teeth."

Jonas chuckles, stepping harder on my ribs until something cracks. "Save it for the pit, sweetheart. My boys'll want to test that filthy little mouth of yours, anyway."

I bite down on my tongue so hard it bleeds, flooding my mouth with copper. Pure agony spreads throughout my chest, but I won't give him the satisfaction of seeing me wince. Instead, I turn my head and chomp down on the closest soldier's wrist, shaking my head side to side until flesh separates from bone.

Blood fills my mouth again, but this time it's not mine. The soldier's scream echoes off the walls as he yanks his arm back with a wet *pop*. I spit a chunk of his skin onto the ground, jaw aching. My lungs heave beneath the boot as I bare my teeth like the rotter I am, aiming my nails toward the other one's eyes before they pin me down once more.

"*Fuck*! The fucker bit me! Has he turned?!"

Jonas removes his boot, replacing it with a knee as he studies me closely. "Nah, he's still in there. But just in case."

Pulling a pistol from his holster, he lifts the gun and pulls the trigger without another word. I flinch, squeezing my lids shut when a body hits the ground beside me, brain matter splattering over my face. Fingers grip my jaw harshly, forcing it apart, and my eyes fly open as Jonas shoves the muzzle of the gun into my mouth.

"You just cost me a good soldier," he spits, close enough to my nose that I gag around the metal invading my throat. "Search the other barrels, see if we got more nasty surprises lurking inside."

"Yes, boss."

Behind him, boots scrape across the floor, the sound of sloshing water filling the space as the others move to obey. My muscles ache, the bitter tang of gunmetal thick on my tongue. I growl around it angrily.

"Still got some fight in him," the woman at my legs mutters.

Jonas hums, patting my cheek roughly. "Bet the freak liked that. Did he fuck you good and hard, rotter? Rip you open with his monster cock?"

"Shit, I'd kill to see that," another soldier groans, gripping his crotch next to my face.

Something sparks in Jonas' eyes, like an idea taking hold, and he yanks the gun from my mouth before standing up. "Come on, then. Flip him over. Let's see how wrecked and sloppy his hole is."

Terror fills my lungs in the form of a scream, reverberating off the walls when they attempt to turn me around. I buck in their grasp, broken ribs burning as my heart races a million miles a minute, but it's no use. Three to one, they pin me on my stomach next to the soldier's corpse, someone's palm pressing my face into the bloody ground. Jonas sits on my thighs, fingers curling into the hem of my pants before yanking them down past my hips. Cold air hits my skin as I holler through my teeth, fighting fruitlessly.

No, no. Not again, please—

The minute they spread my ass apart, I go feral, clawing at the floor until my nails break, but their hold on me won't budge.

"Damn, look at that little thing," Jonas whistles, gripping me tightly. "Either the Ferryman has a tiny prick, or this ass hasn't been properly fucked yet."

"*I'll fucking kill you,*" I snarl, blood and spit flying from my lips.

That only earns me a sharp smack.

"Well, grunt, looks like you got your wish," he chuckles, the sound of a buckle coming undone making me gag. "I'm about to fuck this rotter to death. You can have him after."

"Thanks, boss."

All of the fight evaporates when he spits onto my hole, muscles growing limp. His body lies across my back, pressing me harder into the concrete, making it difficult to breathe. Bile rises into my throat when something nudges my opening, but I can't even brace for the pain that's about to follow because my limbs are no longer my own. They don't move; they don't respond to my brain signals, as if my motor functions have been severed. All I can do is lie here and wait for him to do what he says he's going to do before he kills me.

The corpse's face fills my vision, half his head blown off, but I don't want to see that kind of brutality in my final moments, so I close my eyes. Imagine Charon instead, that kiss beside the waterfall, his fingers brushing over my scars. He's probably pacing the boat right now, waiting for me to come home. His name beats in my chest like a second heartbeat, loud enough that I swear they can probably hear it.

Please, whatever you do, don't come after me. You don't belong here.

The first time I met him, I thought he was the monster, but I was so wrong. It's not him at all.

And then there's *her*. Lena.

My sister's face is blurrier now, fading around the edges, but the sound of her voice is still burned into my bones—*I'll come back for you.*

She said she'd find a way. Said she was working on something big, something that could help us all. But she never came back.

And now, at the end of the road, I'm alone like I've been since the day she left.

Jonas grunts, pulling me out of my thoughts as he grabs my hips, preparing to push forward. I want to shout, to scream at him, tell him to *just get it over with already*—

A loud, screeching caw in the air makes him pause before he can breach me. I glance over my shoulder in time to catch him flinching, eyes jerking upward just as Nyx drops like a curse from the rafters, talons outstretched.

She hits him square in the face, wings flapping wildly across his cheek. He roars, the rifle clattering to the floor beside me as he jumps to his feet, swatting her away.

"GET IT OFF ME!" he bellows, blood pouring from a fresh gash above his brow as Nyx digs in harder, beak snapping dangerously close to his eyes. My captors release me immediately, rushing forward in panic, but she's fury and pure vengeance.

I choke in air, lungs burning as I grab the rifle and roll away, aiming it at the other soldiers before pulling the trigger, spraying bullets with a scream. The weapon jerks violently, nearly dislocating my shoulder, but their bodies hit the ground one after the other.

Nyx's voice cuts through all of the mayhem, raspy and ominous enough to send a chill down my spine. *"Eye for an eye."*

With a shriek that curdles the blood, she dives at Jonas's face again, talons raking down his cheek in perfect precision before her beak plunges into his eye socket.

Jonas's howl is instant. "GET THIS FUCKING BIRD OFF ME—"

There's a wet *pop*, and something round splatters to the ground at my feet, trailing gore.

An eyeball.

He drops to his knees, clutching his face as blood streams through his fingers. "MY FUCKING EYE!"

Nyx launches up, wings snapping out wide. She lands hard on the ground beside me, blood dripping as she picks up the eye and swallows the entire thing whole.

Jonas and I both freeze.

Cocking her head, she turns to me with a proud little puff of her feathers, beak snapping twice. *"Pass."*

Despite everything that just happened, I can't help but bark out a laugh, coughing through the pain when I hold out my arm for her. "Good murder bird."

She hops up happily, talons piercing my skin as she climbs to my shoulder, but the sting is nothing compared to the fury flowing through my veins.

That asshole just tried to stick his cock in me.

Nose-less, *eyeless* son of a bitch.

"Well, well," I drawl, mocking his tone as I get to my knees, the rifle trained on his mutilated face. "Whatever shall we do with you, now?"

CHAPTER EIGHTEEN

Charon

The scent of desperation reaches my nose before the boat even fully stops.

Aster's Hollow sits beneath a layer of fog, smoke curling from the smelter's stacked chimneys. The surrounding water shimmers with traces of oil and ash, clinging to the edges of the dock like rot.

It's quieter than usual. Miners move around like ghosts, their skin pale and sun-starved. A boy, no older than thirteen, drags a rusted ore cart behind him, the wheels groaning eerily.

Near the smoke stack, remnants of an old church still stand, charred and half-collapsed. On its walls, scrawled in thick black paint, are the words, *"O thánatos ta niká óla."*

Death conquers all.

Someone added tally marks beneath it, hundreds or thousands, keeping track of their dead. Somewhere underground, buried in the mines, are miles and miles of graves. Did Hector ever add anyone to those marks? Was there someone here he cared for?

I stay seated near the bow, hunched forward with my arms braced on my knees as the soldiers begin lifting sacks onto the dock. The miners line up on the bank, their faces gaunt and stained with sweat. Most of them are kids.

Rita drops one of the ration bags onto the deck at her feet, kicking it hard. "Our illustrious Judge is in a good mood today. Double supplies to those who produced the most product since our last drop."

My eyes narrow on a young man approaching with a cart full of bullets, silver gleaming beneath layers of soot.

Last time I was here, the soldiers weren't loading silver, they were loading *bodies*. I remember them all herded onto the boat, dirty and hollow-eyed. Petty thieves, runners, those whose age had started to show. Some wept, a few begged for their lives. And in the middle of it all was a small, stubborn man with eyes like forest storms, chin raised in defiance.

Hector.

He hadn't been crying, like most of the others, or bargaining. He'd been *seething*.

It's that look that drew me to him. The defiance behind those eyes, even when a soldier grabbed him by the hair and shoved him onto the boat before knocking him unconscious. That was the moment I noticed him, before he even had a name.

All I can think about is getting back to Zone T, where I hope he'll be waiting for me. Every few seconds, I scan the sky for some sign from Nyx that he's safe.

My knuckles ache from how tightly I've been gripping the rail. The cold bite of salty air does little to clear the storm in my chest that's been growing since the truck carrying Hector disappeared. Every crack and creak of the boat sounds like a warning bell. Too much time has passed.

Rita wipes her forehead with the edge of her sleeve, grinning at the crates of silver bullets and coins. "This lot was better than last time. We should withhold rations more often."

My stomach churns at the thought of these children working themselves to death for things they could easily get themselves, if not for the Judge, but I give her nothing in response.

"We're running behind, let's bring the rest up the coast."

Still, I don't move, just stare out across the muck-slicked water, where the mountains loom in the distance. *Come on, Nyx. Please.*

Rita clicks her tongue but doesn't press further, clearly deeming me not worth her time. The soldiers start piling in, and I finally force myself to my feet with heavy legs. As they secure the supplies in place, I cast one more glance back at Aster's Hollow, at the sagging tents and cracked cabins, the sallow cheeks and bent backs. Every face that boards this boat gets remembered, even if they don't survive long enough to step off it again.

Closing my eyes, I remember Hector's face as he was dragged aboard, the way he looked at the prison walls when he first saw them, as if he was already planning on tearing them down.

That same fire had been in his eyes before he left, locked in that barrel like a secret weapon. Every nerve in my body longs to see him again, to know he's alright.

A flutter of wings cuts through the smog, and my eyes snap open to spot Nyx high above, diving sharply toward me with an anxious caw.

I push past the soldiers and hold out my arm before she lands hard, talons biting into my flesh. Her feathers are ruffled, blood crusted at the edge of her beak.

Her black eyes blink slowly as she cocks her head. *"Gone."*

My blood runs cold, and I stagger back a step, my heart cracking in agony. *No.*

"All gone."

The dock, the crates, the smoke all vanish behind the deafening roar in my ears.

Dead. Hector's dead.

Nyx flutters to my shoulder, but I barely feel her. My knees hit the deck, and I don't even notice until splinters dig into my palms, lungs struggling to work. Rita shouts something, but I can't hear it over my thundering pulse.

He can't be. He was supposed to come back. He *promised.*

A soft croak comes from my shoulder as Nyx nuzzles into my jaw, but I turn my face away. If she saw it with her own eyes...if she's saying it, then it has to be true. She's never lied, not about death.

My chest caves in as the thought slices through me like a blade.

Hector is gone. He's never coming back. *They took another soul from me.*

Rising slowly—too slowly for anyone to notice—my muscles grow taut with rage. Everything turns red as I stare at the soldiers still loading crates onto the boat.

Rita turns just in time to see the look on my face, her brows rising. "Charon?"

I snatch the nearest soldier by the collar and slam his head into the railing so hard his skull cracks. He collapses with a scream as the others scramble, hands reaching for their guns.

Another one rushes me, but I knock the rifle from her hands and drive my fist into her throat, roaring as she crumples to the ground.

"He's gone rogue!"

"What the fuck is happening?!"

Copper floods my mouth, the scent of blood filling the air. Someone yells my name, but it's distant, muffled as I throw a body to the floor and stomp until bones break skin.

They took him from me. The prison. The soldiers. *The Judge.* Just like they've taken everything else. There's nothing left for me in this world.

Two more come at me when I pick up an empty cart, catching one in the head with my swing before an electric shock ripples through my body. They deploy their tasers with enough force to drop me, but I lunge again, only to be hit with another wave of volts that tears a guttural scream from my throat.

I slam against the deck, convulsing as Nyx shrieks in rage above me. She swoops at their faces, but they've outnumbered us.

"Don't shoot! Restrain him!"

Pain blinds me enough that my heart gives a painful thump, knocking me flat on my back. The last thing I see before darkness takes me is the sky above, grey and empty. Void of color or sound, miles of silence stretching overhead. Just like my life.

The world's already forgotten us *both*, and Hector's memory will curse me until my dying breath.

CHAPTER NINETEEN

Hector

The guard's clothes smell like death, but I force myself to breathe through it.

Rough fabric clings to my damp skin, still sticky with dried blood and brain matter. Getting the outfit on had been a hassle with the missing foot, but it fits well enough, surprisingly. Almost like the fates are smiling down at this moment.

"You're going to die," Jonas mutters, one hand clutched to his mangled, bloody eye socket. Nyx watches from a rusted pipe above, keeping the asshole in her sights.

Ignoring him, I finish zipping my coat up and cinch the belt around my waist, adjusting the collar until it hides most of Charon's bite marks. Part of me wishes I didn't have to hide them. If this were another world, another time, I'd wear his brands proudly, claiming him as much as he's claimed me. Maybe someday.

I don't have my cane, and hopping around on one leg isn't exactly ideal, so I improvise. Jonas gapes when I rip one of the belts off a dead soldier and start strapping his rifle to my leg under my pants.

It's not perfect. The barrel digs into my thigh and the handle doesn't fit well in the shoe I've tied to it. Uneven weight makes every step a lurch, but it works and keeps me upright. I can walk. Right now, that's all I need. I just hope I don't shoot myself.

Jonas shifts with a hiss of pain as he tries to get away. I grab his pistol from the holster at my hip and fire at his feet, causing us both to flinch when the bullet ricochets off the concrete and pierces some dirty metal cylinder near a machine.

"There's fucking gas in there, are you insane?!" he bellows, stepping toward a valve, but I cock the gun for another shot like I've seen the soldiers do. Jonas halts at the sound, tossing me a look over his shoulder.

"You're going to help me find my sister," I command, stepping closer with the gun aimed at his face. "And then you're going to get us out of here with enough food for three people."

"They'll kill you before you get past the first checkpoint," he snarls, his remaining eye burning with hatred.

"Then I guess you'd better make sure they don't." Grabbing a mask off one of the corpses, I pull it on to cover my face. "Walk, *boss*. Or I'll let the bird go for your other eye."

Nyx lets out a delighted croak from above, obviously on board with that plan.

"Find Charon," I tell her as I loop my arm with Jonas, pressing the gun to his rib cage. "Tell him I killed them all."

She squawks once before launching into the air with a snap of wings, her silhouette vanishing through a broken window.

Jonas scoffs, his face now completely unrecognizable. "You and that freak are dead as soon as the Judge finds out about this. Worse than dead. I can't wait to watch you get ripped apart in the pit."

I jab the gun into his side roughly, pushing him toward a rusted metal door. "At least you'll be watching with only one eye. I can die peacefully knowing that. Move."

"Ain't nothing peaceful about dying in the pit," he sneers, the door groaning on rusted hinges when he pulls it open. "Think you could survive a horde of biters alone? Doubtful. They'll tear your limbs off while you're still alive and eat them in front of you. That's my favorite part."

"You're fucking sick," I hiss, blinking at those weird flickering ceiling lights as we step out into a narrow, windowless hallway.

Jonas just laughs wickedly. "Go against the Judge and face the consequences. Just ask your freakshow boat operator."

The hallway stretches endlessly, steel doors on either side marked with peeling numbers and yellowed signs I can't read. The deeper we go, the more wrong it feels, like the walls themselves are screaming. "What did Charon do?"

"Fuck if I know. That was before my time, but rumor has it the Ferryman knows a secret he ain't supposed to."

I grip the handgun tighter, pulse thudding in my ears. "A secret?"

Jonas shrugs lazily. "The Judge doesn't like imbalance. You cross the line, you pay the price."

"And Charon paid?

He swings his gaze to mine. "You ever wonder why the freak can't talk?"

My stomach twists into a knot. "He's mute."

"Is he?" Jonas grins, something evil gleaming in his remaining eye.

Suddenly, the silence Charon carries makes me sick, thinking that someone might have done that to him as *punishment.*

I jab the pistol into Jonas's side to keep him moving, filing that information away for later. "My sister, take me to her. She enlisted about ten years ago and I never saw her again. She's called Lena."

Jonas tilts his head, brows jumping high. "That bitch is dead."

"Don't you fucking say that!" With a growl, I slam the gun into his temple, causing him to collapse against the wall. "She's here, I know it. Take me to her. Out of this building, wherever you people live. I'll find her."

He just stares at me briefly, blood dripping down his cheek. "Where we *live?* What do you think this place is, exactly? Is there a pretty little neighborhood in your mind with houses and gardens like the olden days?"

"What the fuck are you talking about? This is a *prison.*"

A lopsided sneer twists his mutilated face, making my stomach turn. "Used to be, back before the world went to Hell. Mega-max for the worst of the worst. Think all of your darkest nightmares come to life. Then the rain began to fall."

It's my turn to stare, swallowing hard. "What does that mean?"

Jonas pushes away from the wall and steps forward until the gun rests flat against his chest. "Stories say the prison held for six weeks...but when the food ran low and the inmates got hungry, what do you think kept them alive?"

"You expect me to believe the guards just let something like that happen?"

He's trying to rattle me, to get inside my head. But there's something in his eye that makes this feel less like a taunt and more like a confession.

"No one *lets* anything happen here. You either adapt, or you end up on the menu."

"That doesn't make any sense!" Grabbing his collar, I shove him forward. "Why would you need to do that when you have all the rations? Isn't that why we mine for silver?"

Jonas chuckles darkly. "Sure, that's the official line, but the Judge doesn't give a fuck about ration tokens."

"Then *why*?"

"I ain't telling you shit, rotter. Just trust me when I say the sister you knew is long fucking gone."

My finger twitches on the trigger. I seriously consider filling this lying asshole's body full of bullets, but then we turn the corner. A sharp snap of electricity buzzes overhead, followed by the low, guttural growl of something...canine.

I freeze instantly.

At the end of the hall, two guards stand beside a thick gate, and between them, three dogs on chains. Big, muscular things, all mottled fur and foamy jowls. Their ears perk at the sight of us. One lets out a low snarl that vibrates in my ribs.

"Keep walking," Jonas mutters. "Act like you belong."

"But I don't," I hiss, suddenly aware of how bad I'm hobbling on the rifle strapped to my leg. "They'll smell it."

"Not if you stop sweating like a guilty fuck."

The guards nod as we approach, their eyes dragging across our clothes, and one of them raises a brow.

"Holy shit, Jonesy, what happened to your face?"

The growling intensifies, claws scraping against concrete.

Jonas grimaces as he gingerly touches his cheek. "The freak's bird attacked me. Took an eye out, too. We're on our way to medical."

"Fuck, I hate that thing. Don't even know why the Judge still lets it live."

"Yeah, well, you know how it goes. Eye for an eye and all that shit."

The biggest dog lunges against its leash, teeth snapping just inches from my hip, and my whole body locks up in fear.

"Got yourself a squirmy one there," the first guard notes dryly, not even moving to help.

Jonas laughs wickedly. "He's scared of dogs, aren't you, *grunt?*"

I say nothing, just nod beneath my mask and keep as far from the beasts as possible.

The guards exchange a look before waving us through. "They catch a whiff of rot, they'll rip right through the chain. Keep him clean."

"Always," he says, yanking me forward by the arm.

Once we're around the corner and out of sight, I finally exhale on wobbling legs.

"You're a shit actor," Jonas chuckles.

"Shut up. Wherever it is you hold people, take me there. Now."

"Sure, sweetheart. It's just beyond this next wing."

I narrow my gaze, dragging him to a stop before we reach the corner. "Why are you helping me?"

He blinks, his one good eye gleaming. "You've got a gun to my ribs and I'm half blind. This ain't help, rotter, it's survival."

"Could've turned me in already," I answer, pointing the gun at his forehead. "Could've screamed for backup. Why haven't you?"

That grin returns, unsettling as it morphs his ruined face. "Maybe I like you. Maybe I want to see how far you'll actually go before you break. Thought it'd be fun to watch."

My grip tightens. "I haven't broken yet."

Could have. So many times in my life, I could have given up, ended it all, put myself out of this misery.

"And that's what makes you interesting," he murmurs before turning down the corridor. "The tougher they are, the louder they scream."

I follow almost mindlessly, reeling slightly from his words. The hallway turns sharply, ending at a sealed door with thick locks and reinforced bars. Jonas punches in a code without me needing to ask, and the mechanism disengages.

"You're not gonna like what you find in here, rotter," he mutters, glancing at me sideways.

"Open it."

The metal groans loudly, almost like this place is warning me not to go any further. But I *have* to, for Lena. So I step through the door with my gun still trained on Jonas, trembling from head to toe.

The smell hits me first—blood, rot, and sweat. Screams echo off the walls, followed by wet snarls and the crack of bone. A large space opens into what used to be a courtyard of some sort, long since gutted and repurposed into a scene straight out of Hell. What remains of the tables have been melted down, welded into a massive cage in the middle of the floor. Nine levels of cells line the walls above, stacked like an audience overlooking the pit. A few heads peek through the bars, watching. Waiting.

And in the center of it all, two figures are locked in a brutal fight under the burning sky.

One is entirely gone, his skin peeling with infection. The other is...still human. Barely. She's missing an eye, wielding a rusted pipe at the biter with all her strength. The swing misses, sending her off balance, and the biter takes advantage by lunging for her shoulder. The crowd watching from their cells cheer, almost like they *want* the girl to die.

Body heat warms my back as Jonas steps in close, his humorless chuckle brushing over my ear.

"Welcome to Zone T. Entertainment for the masses. You win, you get to survive another day. But if you lose..." He shrugs, gesturing to a shredded corpse hanging from a hook near the far wall. "Well. Waste not, want not. Everything gets repurposed."

The acid rising in my throat finally spills over, and I bend to vomit onto the ground, barely feeling Jonas press his stiff cock into my ass.

"You do this to rotters?" I choke, vision blurring.

He groans when another scream rips through the air, hands tightening on my hips. "Potential soldiers, too. Everyone serves their time in the pit."

My heart pounds in my ears as the woman shrieks for help, her arm completely separated from her body. The soldiers just laugh, a few of them with their cocks out, making my stomach roil again in horror.

Somewhere in this circle of Hell could be my sister. Somewhere in those cells, maybe one of the guards patrolling above.

I don't know anything anymore, but I do know this:

The inferno awaits, and I'm walking straight into the flames.

CHAPTER TWENTY

Hector

Misery clings to the air, choking my lungs as I move past the cells on the highest level. Getting up all those stairs took most of my strength, but there are fewer soldiers up here to witness what I'm doing.

The enclosures are cramped, maybe five feet wide, and sealed by reinforced doors with portholes barely the size of a dinner plate. Some are dark, others aren't. I force myself to look inside each one.

"Lena?" I call quietly, dragging my palm along the rusted metal while I limp my way around. "Lena, it's me. It's Hector."

Most of the people inside don't answer. A few do, begging for mercy. Blank stares greet me, faces so hollow I don't even recognize them as human at first. One woman reaches for me, fingertips raw and bloody, but she's too far gone to speak. Another hisses and recoils, curling in on herself. These aren't just prisoners...they're ghosts. Shells of who they used to be.

"We put the rotters up here," Jonas says quietly, swirling his finger lazily around a lock. "Keeping them behind steel doors in case they turn. Also makes it convenient if you want some privacy."

I tear my gaze away from a wraith-like form on the floor. "Lena isn't a rotter. She came here to be a soldier."

"Hmm." He examines his nails with a bored shrug. "Guess we could check the list for her name."

My gaze flies to his face, heart skipping a beat. "There's a list?"

"Everyone gets cataloged, sweetheart. Blood types, infection markers. Useful skills. It's all very organized."

"Why the fuck didn't you tell me?!" I snarl, slamming him against the wall before shoving the handgun under his chin. "Why would you bring me all the way up here?"

"Watching you squirm is so much fun," Jonas laughs, unfazed by the metal digging into his jaw.

Rage tunnels my vision, finger tightening on the trigger. "Tell me where it is before I paint the walls with what's left of your face."

He bites his bottom lip as if holding back a grin. "Judge's office. Feel free to check it without me. You've got about five minutes before the next rotation, though, so I'd hustle."

I shove away with a growl, knocking him sideways before bolting for the stairwell. My heart pounds at my ribs, but just as I reach the railing, movement across the pit catches my eye. Two soldiers drag someone to a lower level—a large man.

They haul him like dead weight, one of them unlocking a cell while the other slams the man against the bars hard enough to make me flinch. My knees nearly give out when I recognize the broad chest, blood-smeared skin, and dark hair matted to his forehead.

Charon.

They throw him into the cell like trash, slamming the bars shut tight. My stomach drops at the sight of him slumped on the floor.

Why is he here? Where's Nyx?

Jonas steps up beside me, nursing his jaw with a smirk. "Well, this is perfect." His eye swings to me, glittering darkly. "Think he'll like watching me fuck all of your holes in the pit before we let the biters take you apart?"

I don't even look at him. My gaze stays on Charon, on the way his arms sprawl out unnaturally like they couldn't even bother being gentle with the giant who showed so much kindness to me. My nails dig into my palms hard enough to cut skin as I blink rapidly.

"You gonna cry, rotter? Beg me to set your boyfriend free?"

"I'm not begging," I whisper, jabbing my gun once more into his ribs. "Now take me to the list."

First Lena. Then Charon. I can do this.

Jonas leans in, lips brushing my ear, making me gag. "You're not begging *yet.*" He passes me on the stairs, whistling a tune like this is just another day for him. "But you will be. Very soon."

The halls grow quieter the further we get from the pit, lights humming faintly above. Jonas walks a few steps ahead, casually swinging his arms back and forth. It seems...cleaner here, somehow. Less grime and decay on the walls. I don't like it one bit.

"The Judge's office is just ahead," he says flatly. "Real charming place. Great view of the shit-filled swamp surrounding us."

"Walk faster."

He snorts but complies, swaggering up to another door with a keypad. "If I weren't so excited to have you in the pit, I'd almost regret that our fun is about to end. As it were..."

The door unlocks with a sharp hiss before swinging open quietly, no hinges groaning or rusted metal flaking. Inside, the room looks immaculate. Metal walls, a bolted desk, and odd blinking rectangles lining the far wall that resemble moving pictures. Filing cabinets sit behind the desk, intact and free of dirt, unlike the ones I've seen back in Aster's Hollow.

Jonas throws himself into a chair, leg slung over the arm. "Catalog's somewhere around here. Good luck."

Without hesitating, I immediately pull open the closest drawer to rifle through, hoping *something* will pop out at me. But all I see are words and symbols that I never learned to read. The labels are faded, crumbling papers crammed into folders and loose sheets layering the bottom. My fingers tremble as I flip through them, heart pounding louder with every useless page I toss aside. Compared to how neat the rest of the office is, something about this mess bothers me. It doesn't make sense.

"Where is she?" Scanning a list of numbers that mean nothing to me, I move to the next cabinet, and the next, but there's *noth-*

ing I can understand. Panic rises in my throat at the thought of Charon still in that cell.

Jonas clicks his tongue, breath suddenly hot on my neck. "Having trouble?"

Spinning around, I jam the gun into his throat, forcing him back. "Tell me where the fuck to find the list!"

"Maybe there isn't one," he sneers, empty eye socket oozing and swollen. "Maybe I lied. Maybe your sister never made it off the freak's boat. You ever think of that?"

"Shut up."

"Touched a nerve, hm?"

I plant my hand on his chest and shove him so hard that he falls onto the desk, a maniacal laugh leaving his lips. "This doesn't make any sense!"

She *enlisted*. I watched her leave with my own eyes. She *promised* she'd come back for me. If she's not here, then...where else could she be?

"Why don't you just ask the Judge yourself?" Jonas chuckles, leaning on his elbows.

My gaze snaps to him, blood roaring in my ears. "What did you say?"

"You wanna know what happened to your sister?" He lifts a hand, gesturing toward the door with a crooked finger. "Then ask her yourself."

The lock clicks behind me.

Turning slowly, my heart pounds so loud I almost don't hear the footsteps approach. But when the door swings open, I swear all the air leaves the room.

She stands there, backlit by harsh light, every inch of her now a stranger—worn boots, regulation jacket, her blonde curls cut short. No trace of softness remains in the curve of her silver-scarred mouth.

But I know that face. I know *her*. I could never forget.

A cruel smile spreads on Lena's lips, eyes that used to shine with fondness now colder than the harshest winter as she points a gun straight at my heart.

"Hello, little brother."

CHAPTER TWENTY-ONE

Charon

"Read with me."

Mother's soft voice draws me away from the screams echoing below.

I crawl across the creaky mattress without hesitation, curling beside her in the narrow cot we're not supposed to share. Her fingers are cracked from scrubbing the floors, but when she opens the worn leather book on her lap, they hold steady.

It's the only book left. There used to be more, but he destroyed them all.

She starts to read as I lean on her shoulder, following the page with my eyes. The words don't make a lot of sense yet, but she turns them into music. My fingers trace the lines as she sings them in my ear.

A door slams down the corridor, making us both flinch. Her thumb tightens on the page, but she only reads louder, like maybe the words will keep the monsters out.

"He'll never hurt you," she murmurs when the chapter ends, brushing my hair back to repeat the words she scrawled in the corner of her book. "Not while I'm here. I'll protect you for as long as I breathe."

The lights flicker above as boots stomp toward us, and I know what's coming before he enters the cell. But I don't want to go. I don't want to fight in the pit again.

I don't want to be the monster he's making me into.

My mother's grip tightens when the bars slide open, but it doesn't stop him from yanking me out of her arms.

"Charon, remember who you are. Remember who you are!"

Her screams still echo in my nightmares.

Remember, remember, remember...

Remember.

A flutter of wings pulls me out of the dream.

Something cold brushes my cheek, a sharp nip not quite hard enough to draw blood. With a strained exhale, I blink through the pounding in my skull as the world shifts into focus—the bars, the damp stone floor, the sharp ache in my ribs.

I don't remember how I got here—just pain, and agony, followed by the cold embrace of darkness.

Nyx sits on my chest, head tilted with one beady eye staring into mine urgently. When I don't move fast enough, she hops up onto my collarbone and pecks at my jaw again.

"*Pass,*" she croaks impatiently.

I drag myself upright slowly, breathing through my nose as the air shifts, thick with the scent of blood. A choked sob leaves my throat when I recognize where I am.

The pit. Zone T. Down below, guards pace while two rotters battle it out for food. My stomach turns at the screams, echoing the same as they did back then, and I drop my face into my hands. Just like that, I see my mother again. Not in the flesh, not now, but in the memory I've buried so deep it rips my heart clean from my chest.

She'd been standing in the center of the pit, blood dripping down her face. He threw her in there—the one they called the Judge. My father.

He'd said she was too soft, that her love made me weak. She wasn't immune like me. She'd never survive in the pit. I remember shouting for her as he'd held me down, forcing me to watch her die.

But it wasn't biters she'd been facing.

No, it was *her.*

Lena.

Hector's sister killed my mother and took her place.

The memory fades, but the ache it leaves behind claws at my ribs. I curl my fingers into my hair, nails biting into my scalp as the echo of her victory shout rings in my ears.

She looked right at me after she did it, holding my mother's head high. They'd dragged me away screaming. That was the last time I spoke to anyone, other than Nyx.

I'd found her the very next day on the dock, sick and unable to fly. She was small then, one wing dragging uselessly along the dirt. Wouldn't eat. So I'd cupped her in my hands and carried her back to my cell, naming her after my mother.

She'd learned my voice before I lost it. Every word I spoke to her, every soft murmur to keep myself from breaking, even when Lena demanded we use the crow for testing the infected after taking my voice from me.

And now she's taken Hector, too.

Nyx flutters from my shoulder to the bars, her beak clicking as she glances back at me with an impatient caw. I lift my head and huff at her, yanking on the bars to show her that I'm *trapped*.

Her wings snap open with a hiss of air as she launches herself up into the shadows, disappearing just as heavy boots thump down the corridor. A guard strolls past the cell, chewing on something, and his lip curls when he sees me.

"Well, look at the freak, all locked up tight," he sneers, leaning closer to the bars. "Thought you were tough, but this place breaks everyone eventually, huh?"

Tilting my head, I let him ramble as Nyx drops silently from the rafters above, completely unseen by the arrogant bastard.

But I see her just fine.

And I smile darkly.

With a sharp shriek, she dives for his head. The guard barely has time to gasp before claws rake across his face, tearing through flesh and eyes. He stumbles back, swatting wildly at the air as blood spatters the wall. She plunges again, this time straight for the key ring at his hip, and by the time he fumbles for his weapon, it's too late. She yanks the ring free before flinging it through the bars with a triumphant caw, where they clatter to the floor beside me.

I flip through the keys quickly, already knowing what to look for from years of walking this prison myself.

Click.

When the bars slide open, I'm on him in an instant, wrapping my fingers around his throat. The guard tries to fight, but he's too weak as I crush his windpipe beneath my hands.

Nyx flutters onto the ground beside me, blood still streaking her feathers. She watches me grab the guard's gun before slumping against the wall, chest heaving in agony.

He's gone. Hector was mine, and she took him, just like she's taken everything else.

My gaze darts toward the walkway ahead, then down to the pit where the soldiers claim a victor. I need to move, to get away, but...*I don't want to*, not without him.

If I stay here, I'll die. If I run, I'll still probably die, just a little slower. But maybe I can make my death actually *mean* something.

And when I finally see Hector again in Elysium, I can greet him proudly.

Nyx caws quietly, nudging the keys toward my boot as if she can read my thoughts. I pick them up slowly, formulating my plan. They jingle in my grip, metal slick with blood as I move down the corridor and up to the top level, screams echoing somewhere below.

First door on the left, I pause.

Inside, a woman sits curled in the corner, wrists raw from the silver cuffs. Her eyes track me as I open the door and unlock her shackles. She doesn't move at first, but I leave her for the second cell. Then the third. Some of them are too far gone to register what's happening, others blink like the light burns after so long in the dark. One man starts sobbing, falling to his knees.

"Thank you, thank you," he sobs into my hand.

I continue on.

Down and down I go, opening doors, letting every forgotten soul free. By the time I reach the last level, the hall behind me is full of murmurs and shuffling feet. I press my back to the wall, meeting their hopeful stares as Nyx lands on my shoulder with a satisfied ruffle of her feathers.

She understands what we have to do.

The match has been lit, and now all that's left is to watch this place burn.

CHAPTER TWENTY-TWO

Hector

"N*o.*" I stumble back, knocking into the edge of the desk. "You...can't be. This isn't real."

Her grip on the gun doesn't falter. "I am. And it is."

Jonas lets out a harsh chuckle. "I knew this would be an exciting reunion."

My head whips toward him as I aim for his head with a snarl. "You fucking *knew* she was the Judge from the start!"

"Of course I did. Who do you think promoted me? Lena has her favorites, and I'm a *very* loyal dog."

My sister readies her gun, the click echoing off the walls. "Put it down, Hector."

I meet her cold gaze, heart hammering in my ribs. "You'd shoot your own brother?"

"If you don't lower your weapon, I will."

A rough, disbelieving laugh claws its way up my throat. "Do you have *any* idea what this asshole did? He had your guards hold me down while he tried to force his cock into me!"

"Damn bird had to ruin the fun," Jonas mumbles, but not before something flashes in Lena's eyes.

"Either you drop the gun and kick it over, or I'll shoot."

Everything tilts around me as the sharp edge of her words scrapes something raw inside my chest.

My sister. My *fucking* sister is the Judge. Ruler over this place of horrors where people suffer, where the guards kill and maim and rape.

I lower the gun slightly, more out of shock than anything else. "What the hell happened? You...you said you were leaving to make things better. You said you'd come back for me."

Lena's jaw tightens, scar stretching thin across her lips. "I did come back. Just...not in the way you expected."

"That's bullshit! You disappeared. I waited for *years*, Lena. You promised—"

"I promised a lot of things," she cuts in. "I was naïve then, but you're still alive, aren't you? You survived."

"*Survived?*" My hands start to tremble violently around the pistol. "You left me to starve. I was a *child*."

She looks at me then, *really* looks at me. Her gaze jumps from the bruises on my throat to the crooked lean of my gait. "You don't know what I've done to keep us alive."

Taking a slow step forward, the gun falls limply at my side. "So tell me what's happening. Tell me why you hurt Charon!"

"Not until you hand over your weapon."

Jonas hums, glancing between us in amusement. "This is about to get good."

She doesn't even look at him. "I'm giving you a choice, Hector. Listen to me or die in the pit. You decide."

All I can do is stare in disbelief, breathing heavily.

Listen to her? After everything? After what she did to Charon and me? To all these people trapped here? My limbs refuse to move.

Lena keeps her gun trained on me, but her grip is shaky. She's waiting to see what I'll do. Jonas tenses as well, bracing for a fight, but I realize I'm outnumbered. I couldn't fight them both off with one foot, and I don't even know if I have bullets left.

So I make my choice, despite every instinct screaming not to.

Slowly, I crouch as much as I can, setting the gun on the ground with a quiet *clack*.

Jonas lets out an exaggerated sigh of disappointment. "Fucking buzzkill."

My sister studies me with a stern gaze, her jaw relaxing. She finally lowers her weapon just enough to make it clear that she's not shooting me yet. "Get up."

Gripping my leg, I rise with a glare, never taking my eyes off her.

"Walk," she says, gesturing for me to precede her into the hall. The barrel of her weapon presses into my spine as I limp past.

"I get him when you're finished, right?" Jonas asks, hanging back in the doorway. "I called dibs."

"Get back to your post, Jonas," she snaps, nudging me forward. "And check on that fucking gas leak."

"Yes, ma'am."

My pulse thuds behind my eyes, the hallway narrower somehow, like the walls are closing in around me. We walk for a long, silent moment, Lena's boots echoing steadily at my back.

"Left," she orders suddenly, and I turn at the next junction, passing more doors until she tells me to stop.

Another keypad, another code. She types it in, then a low mechanical clunk makes me flinch as the door unlatches and we step inside.

I barely have time to take in my surroundings before the gun clatters to the ground as she *yanks me into her arms.*

"Fucking hell, I missed you," she chokes, squeezing me hard enough that my ribs ache. "I never thought I'd see you again."

I freeze in her grasp, too stunned to react. "You pointed a gun at me five minutes ago."

Lena pulls away just enough to look me in the eye, her lashes wet. "And you were pointing one at my second-in-command. I had to keep up appearances."

Finally, my brain catches up with the situation, and I shove her off me with a snarl. "*Appearances?* I've been right where you left me the whole time! Starving and alone and rotting!"

My sister opens her mouth, the tough mask cracking as something trembles behind her eyes. "I did what I had to," she finally says, rolling her shoulders. "I couldn't come back. Not yet. Not until I had something to offer."

"Like what? A horde of soldiers who beat and rape people for fun?"

Her expression hardens again, the silver scar over her lips twisting grotesquely. "I don't expect you to understand. You've only seen pieces of this place. Shadows. You don't know what it's like here."

I want to believe her. Fuck, I do, but I've seen the pit. I've seen the cells. It makes me want to scream, to hit something, to hit *her*. But I just stand there, trembling, because I don't know which version of her is real—the sister I loved or this monster she's become.

"You want answers?" she says, walking deeper into the room. "Then let me explain. I'll tell you everything."

My stomach drops when I gaze after her, finally focusing on where we are. Some kind of crude lab sits against the far wall, pieced together with rusted metal counters and beeping machines I can't process.

But that's not what causes my breath to catch in my throat.

It's the *creature* strapped to a steel table, barely conscious, limbs bound with leather belts. It looks almost human, veins vibrantly blue beneath thin, papery skin. Next to it on a metal tray are vials and syringes.

"What the fuck is this?" I whisper, rearing back.

Lena doesn't even flinch as she makes her way over to the tray. "Research. The infection started somewhere, and that means it can end somewhere, too."

I choke out a gasp, unable to tear my gaze from the poor soul on the table. Its scalp bleeds beneath clumps of hair, flesh peeling away from the bone. "You're *torturing* people?"

"I'm trying to save them," she snaps as she lifts a syringe. "This is how we do it, Hector. You'll see."

Before I can even blink, she plunges a needle into the creature's neck

It lets out a shriek loud enough to hurt my ears as its body arches against the restraints, foam spilling from its gaping mouth. The stench of metal hits my nostrils.

"Silver," she says calmly, watching her victim writhe. "We think it slows the cellular breakdown, stabilizes the brain for a while. Sometimes they even talk."

The creature lets out a gurgling moan that sounds almost like a word. I stagger back with a gagging dry heave.

My sister strokes the thing's cheek almost reverently, even as it snaps its teeth at her. "This one used to run the place. The original 'Judge'. He never believed in what I'm doing here, so I had to make him *see*."

"You're insane," I growl, swallowing down my rising nausea.

"I'm desperate," she snaps. "You think I like this? I'm doing what no one else had the strength to do, what no one *believed* could be done."

"All you're doing is hurting people!" Turning toward the door, I try to pull on the handle, but it won't budge. "Let me go. I need to find Charon. I don't want any part in your psycho experiments."

"I'm trying to cure you, Hector!" she yells, her voice breaking on my name.

My hand falls away from the handle as I throw her a glance over my shoulder, brows furrowing. "There's no cure. Everyone knows that."

She yanks down her shirt collar, revealing a glistening silver bite mark on her shoulder. "I found one. At least, a suppressant, anyway."

"What...what happened?"

Something haunted shifts in her gaze. "I was working in the mine with our father. He turned into a biter with no warning, attacking me out of the blue. I didn't even have time to think, I just grabbed the closest thing I could find."

Her eyes glaze over as she continues, "It was a silver pickaxe. I buried it in his heart and watched his body seize like it was on fire. But then, as he bled out on the floor, his face changed. Suddenly, the snarling biter was gone, and he was Father again. He lived long enough to say he was sorry before he died."

My back hits the wall, vision going dim. "You're lying. He left us!"

"No, that's just the excuse I came up with. You were a kid, you wouldn't have understood."

"I waited for him," I whisper, sinking to my knees as my legs give out. "I used to sleep by the front door in case he came back."

"I know." She smiles at me sadly. "And I let you believe it because the truth would've destroyed you."

"It did destroy me. I thought...I thought he hated me for being...rotten."

Lena drops her gaze then. For a long moment, all I can hear is the wet breaths of that thing on the table and my heart pounding in my ears. Eventually, she continues.

"After he was gone, I ran into town. Told everyone I could find about what happened, even the soldiers, but no one believed me.

They all thought I was crazy. So I decided to enlist instead and bring it up to the man in charge."

She begins to pace frantically, the thud of her boots hollow. "He laughed at me. Told me silver was too precious to be wasted on theories, and if I wanted to be useful, I'd put my mouth to work."

My fingers curl into the floor, nails scraping against the concrete as I inch for the gun she'd dropped.

"But I didn't shut up. I spent four years in his bed, gathering allies to my side. Even killed the Ferryman's mother for a spot in the guard."

The breath catches in my lungs at the mention of Charon's past.

"He didn't expect me to win," she laughs maniacally. "But I *did*. I killed her, Hector, and then I made this place my own."

"What did you do to Charon?" I rasp, chest heaving as I struggle to breathe through her explanations.

She steps slowly to the table, putting distance between us as the creature sobs softly. "The people at Aster's Hollow would have never followed me. They respected the Judge too much to listen to some girl. So I kept the miners believing he was still in charge, convincing them that the river had tainted all the plants and animals, and made everyone depend on me for food. The soldiers follow so long as I let them do what they want, and in exchange, I get to test the silver on them. It's become a game. Whoever can withstand the most pain gets bumped up in my ranks."

I swallow past the horror in my throat as her words settle into place. "And Charon?"

Lena's gaze flicks to mine for a heartbeat before darting away again. "He knew the truth, little brother, so I gave him a choice. Join me or don't. He hated the fact that I took his mommy's place, so he refused."

"So you took his voice?" My stomach burns from how hard I try not to vomit.

"I spared his life," she snaps, turning to me with wild eyes. "I nearly severed his jugular in the pit, but if it weren't for the fact that he's immune, he'd be dead by now! I needed his blood."

"You experimented on him." Rage sears through me as I struggle to a stand.

Her mouth twists, silver scar catching the light as she snarls, "I had to. He's immune, Hector. Do you have any idea how rare that is? I couldn't just waste him when his blood could hold the key to saving you!"

"What did you do to him, Lena?"

She exhales irritably, like I'm dragging this out for no reason. "I started small. Drew his blood, mixed it with powdered silver, tested it on prisoners who'd just been bitten. Nothing. So I tried injecting the silver directly into his veins, watched him shake and sweat and choke it down. He survived every dose."

I bite my tongue so hard that copper floods my mouth. "And then?"

"I let the biters feed from him," she says matter-of-factly. "Not enough to kill him, but enough to give them a taste. I wanted to see if his immunity mixed with silver could burn the infection out from the inside." Her eyes go distant, like she's replaying it in her head. "Some of them lasted hours before turning. Some screamed for days on end. But none of them survived."

"You hurt the one person who's ever truly cared about me." The gun trembles in my hands as I struggle to breathe.

"He helped his father run this prison before me. You think he did any better? At least I gave people something to believe in."

"You gave them something to fear. There's a difference." The creature behind her lets out a weak cry, and I know—I just *know*—that Charon was strapped to that same table once. Maybe more than once.

My grip tightens on the gun. "You keep saying this was all for me, but the only person you're trying to save is yourself. What are you gonna do, Lena, throw me in the pit? *Experiment* on me? Let Jonas have his way?"

"I'd never let them hurt you!" she snarls, outraged.

"You already did!" My voice bounces off the walls with the force of my shout. "You left me alone to defend myself, and you know what your soldiers did to me? What they did to a starving *child* caught in the woods? There are times I wish they'd killed me."

Her whole body jerks like I slapped her, and for one brief second, she doesn't look like the Judge. She just looks like Lena. My sister. The girl who used to braid my hair while humming off-key and make shadow puppets on the wall every night.

But that girl is gone.

"I told you to stay out of the woods," she mumbles, blinking rapidly. "I didn't know that they'd—"

"Oh, *bullshit*." I cut her off with a harsh laugh. "You knew exactly what monsters you created. You've known all along. But you needed them, right? Just like you needed the pit and the silver. The *bodies*."

She's shaking now, eyes glassy as they scan my face. "I didn't have a choice."

"You had a thousand choices, and every time, you *didn't pick me.*"

Silence coils between us as the whimpering behind her grows louder. Lena opens her mouth, but only air comes out as her jaw quivers. "I'm sorry. If I had known what they'd done to you…"

"Don't pretend this would've gone any different if you had."

She flinches, a tear slipping down her cheek, but it does nothing to sway me. Not now.

Her feet move as she steps forward, arms outstretched, but the creature on the table jerks suddenly, a guttural scream tearing from its throat.

We both freeze.

It breaks its restraints in a sudden, violent snap, the leather shredding beneath frantic limbs. Lena barely has time to scream before it lunges, no longer human as it sinks its rotting teeth into her neck.

"Lena!" I shout, instinctively raising the gun to shoot.

"Hector, wait! There's gas—"

The minute my finger pulls the trigger, a blinding light flashes in the air.

Then fire.

Heat sears my face as the blast throws me through the door, my body slamming into the wall hard enough to wind me. The entire room erupts into flame as the roof blows open, an inferno raging through the corridor.

My ears ring loudly, drowning out the screams as I cough, trying to breathe and clear my vision.

By the time the smoke dissipates, I see nothing left of my sister.

Just burning wreckage and blackened corpses slumped beneath the rubble.

CHAPTER TWENTY-THREE

Charon

At first, every prisoner remains frozen in fear.

I get it. Freedom doesn't come easy in a place built to break you, and I know what it's like to sit so long in the dark that you forget the shape of the sun.

"*Good to go,*" Nyx croaks, flapping her wings as she launches into the air.

Someone screams in the pit, followed by the sound of soldiers *laughing.* A woman steps up to the railing, bony fingers curling around the rusted metal as she gazes down at the scene below. A single tear tracks down her cheek.

"*You're free,*" I whisper, though I'm sure she can't hear.

But she seems to understand all the same. Her gaze cuts to mine in gratitude before she steps onto the stairs, and someone follows. Then another, and another.

A ripple of motion rolls down the walkway as everyone moves, stretching and breathing like they haven't in years. The forgotten, the discarded, the ones left here to rot. Just like Hector and me.

Not anymore.

Rage that has festered beneath my skin for ten long years finally roars to the surface as I follow them down. Prisoners pour from their cells, half-starved but thirsty, eager for blood.

They called us monsters, treated us like beasts. Now they'll see what monsters *really* look like.

The guards barely have time to raise their weapons before we storm the pit. One of them swings a bat in my direction, but I catch it mid-air, twisting his wrist until it snaps before shoving him hard into the crowd. They take him apart piece by piece, bludgeoning him with his own weapon.

"Don't shoot! Don't shoot!" Rita tries to rally her men on one of the upper levels, aiming her baton toward the mass of bodies rushing forward. "I said hold your fucking fire, we've got a gas leak!"

A boulder of a man barrels into her from the side, driving her body over the edge, and her scream cuts off in a sickening crunch.

A killing calm takes over my senses. Leaping over the railing, my feet hit the ground in the pit with a *crack*, knees absorbing the shock as more prisoners follow. Blood splatters my face when I rip a blade from a guard's belt before driving it into his stomach, intestines splashing to the floor.

Cheers ring out from the cells above. Soldiers rush through the open doors, but there are more of us than there are of them, and they can't get control without their guns.

Just as I drive my fist into someone's face, a thunderous *BOOM* shakes the ground beneath my boots. Shockwaves ripple through the compound when a fireball bursts skyward from the western wing, sending stone and dust raining down. Terrified screams follow the blast.

I stagger back, nearly losing my balance as I whip toward the noise, heart thundering wildly. The power flickers, lights sputtering before dimming to a red glow as sirens begin to sound above the chaos. Emergency mode.

"Fucking die!" A guard lunges at me from behind, but one of the prisoners tackles him to the ground, sinking his teeth into the man's throat.

Snarling barks reach my ears as a body falls from the upper level, but not even their dogs are enough to hold us back.

The pit has become a battlefield. Smoke chokes the air as sweat, metal, and burning flesh coat my tongue. A woman runs past, wielding a leg like a weapon, laughing maniacally when she slams it into someone's head. Searing pain runs down my shoulder from a stray blade, but I don't fall, diving low to sweep a guard's legs from beneath him before pounding my fists into his face again and again until he stops twitching.

"In we go!" Nyx shrieks above the bloodbath, her swooping shadow pulling me out of my haze. She lands on my shoulder, cawing once before launching back into the ashes toward the western wing. Toward *Lena,* and the place where she took everything from me.

I take off after her, each step sending fire through my legs, but I don't slow down. The hallway is a blur of carnage—bodies litter the floor, guards and prisoners both, the dead indistinguishable from the dying. Someone grabs for me, but I shake them off, barely noticing the way their blood smears my arm.

Nyx dips down again at the corridor split, screaming over her shoulder before vanishing. My boots skid through ash and soot as I follow, chest burning from the smoke, fury tangled in my lungs. I skid to a stop when I spot the doors blown wide open, one hanging crooked on its hinges, the other scorched black. A pipe hisses steam into the hall as someone screams, making me jolt, because it sounds like *Hector*. Has the bloodlust driven me mad already?

Pain explodes in my ribs when a guard slams into my back, tackling me into the wall. The impact knocks the breath out of me. My shoulders spasm in pain, but I snarl through it, grabbing his wrist as he raises a blade. The knife slices along my arm, burning hot, but it's not deep enough to stop me as my elbow connects with his jaw.

He stumbles, blood spraying from his mouth. I shove him down and grab the knife, jamming it into his neck over and over and *over* until it completely severs the bone.

Once the body stills beneath me, I sag over it, blinking blood from my lashes. Adrenaline surges through my veins, the rhythm of my heart painfully tight. I can hardly breathe.

Nyx screeches again, drawing my attention. When I look ahead to find her, all of my strength leaves my limbs, because I see *him*.

Not clearly—not yet—but the unmistakable figure stepping from the mouth of the corridor could be no one else.

Smoke curls around him, clothes torn and dirty, but his face...

His face is everything.

It takes me a several seconds to believe this is real, that I haven't broken so completely that my mind is crafting phantoms just to keep me moving. But then his wide emerald eyes find mine, and my blood roars to life inside my veins.

I rise to my feet, barely noticing the gore dripping from my arms or the taste of copper on my tongue. There is nothing in this moment except *him*.

Hector. Beautiful, frightened, covered in soot, but *alive*.

And I'll never let anyone take him from me again.

CHAPTER TWENTY-FOUR

Hector

He's drenched in blood.

Crimson stains his hands and arms, soaking into the fabric that clings to his frame like a second skin. A guard at his feet isn't moving, head separated from the body. The Ferryman stands over it like a god of death, shoulders heaving and eyes wild.

But I'm not afraid.

My instincts don't scream *run*. My heart doesn't twist in fear. If anything, it slows, because despite the carnage unfolding around us, I've never felt safer than I do at this moment. Even standing before him after he just murdered someone in cold blood.

"Charon," I whisper, barely able to get his name past the rawness in my throat.

He takes a step forward, and another, eyes never leaving my face. When he finally draws near, he picks me up, strong arms wrapping around my waist so tight I can barely breathe.

"You came for me," I choke, touching my forehead to his.

Charon's breath shudders against my face, body trembling as guttural sobs claw at his throat.

I press my lips to his cheek, threading my fingers through his blood-matted strands. "It's okay. I'm here now, we're okay."

He simply nods, kissing each of my eyelids as his grip on me tightens, and my heart breaks at the anguish on his face. His nose brushes mine before he leans in, resting his cheek against my shoulder with ragged, uneven breaths. We stay suspended in time until the sirens outside the corridor yank us back to reality.

"Charon, we have to move."

He huffs against my shoulder, but when he pulls back, he doesn't let me go.

"I can walk—" I protest, even as my ruined leg throbs.

He only taps his forehead to mine for a fleeting second before stepping forward, my weight nothing in his arms.

So I rest my head against his neck, inhaling the sweat and blood as he carries me back toward the scorched hallway where my sister just died and everything changed.

The air is thick with smoke, walls black and bleeding ash. Charon's steps slow as we pass the door still hanging off its hinges. Heat pulses out in suffocating waves when we stop to peer inside the obliterated room.

Shrapnel embeds the walls, concrete floor cracked. What's left of my sister is unrecognizable, just scraps of fabric and silver glinting amid the debris.

I wish I could feel something.

Grief. Anger. Closure.

But all I feel is numb.

"You knew she was the Judge," I whisper.

He pauses, then lifts one hand to cup the back of my head, turning my face to his. Those blue eyes bore into mine sadly, his lips parting as he mouths an apology.

I'm sorry.

"You don't need to be," I murmur, turning back to gaze at her blackened corpse. "She made her choice."

So did I.

The Ferryman carries me past it all, into whatever future we're bleeding toward, the fire behind us casting long shadows on the path ahead. Sirens keep blaring, but no echo of gunshots trail us.

Up ahead, Nyx seems to lead the way, banking around a corner toward Lena's office, where the door still stands open from when she marched me out at gunpoint.

We step through the threshold, ducking slightly so I don't knock into the frame. He sets me down gently on the edge of the desk before kneeling between my knees, his eyes and hands roaming my body for signs of damage.

"What now?" I ask, the sirens muffled this far into the building.

He just continues his assessment with a shake of his head, not meeting my gaze.

Nyx flutters onto the windowsill, tapping her beak against the glass with a pointed look in our direction. Beyond it, all I see is miles of polluted water.

"Do you know a way out?"

Again, just a shake of the head. When his touch runs across my thighs, I shiver, instinctively grabbing his wrists to keep his palms in place.

He goes still, gaze finally meeting mine. I run my fingers up his bloody arms, tracing old bite marks along his flesh. "Did she do this to you?"

He doesn't shake his head this time, but he doesn't nod, either. His throat bobs with a hard swallow as I ghost my lips over the jagged scar on his neck.

"It's okay," I murmur, even though it isn't. "You don't have to tell me."

Charon shifts a hand to my hip, the other curling around the back of my neck. We move in tandem, both leaning in to press our mouths together in the softest kiss, and it's like a dam breaks inside of me.

After everything that has happened, the stories I've heard and the brutality I've witnessed, the tenderness in his touch is enough to shatter my thundering heart.

Grabbing his torn shirt, I pull him closer to deepen the kiss as my legs wrap around his waist. A slight breath leaves his lungs, and when his tongue traces the seam of my lips, I open for him, too far gone to care about the blood still coating his skin.

The warmth of his body between my legs is overwhelming, the desperate tremble in his hands as they cradle my face. I claw at his shirt in a frenzy to rip it off, the fabric tearing easily. My palms run down the hair dusting his chest, sweeping over his abs to the hem of his pants while I suck on his tongue, my cock growing heavy and stiff.

In the back of my mind, something screams at me to slow down, that we're in danger and covered in blood, but it only makes me *hungrier* for him. Judging by how hard he is when I slip my hand beneath his waistband, I'd say the Ferryman feels the same.

Charon breaks our kiss first, leaning his forehead against mine with a shaky exhale as he thrusts into my palm, eyes closed and lips swollen. He looks so damn beautiful that I don't look away, wanting to remember this moment in case we don't make it until morning.

I wish I'd met him sooner.

"Let go," I say quietly, stroking his cock with the rhythm of my pulse, savoring the way his fingers tighten in my curls. "It's okay. Let go for me."

His whole body tenses, muscles pulled taut as a bowstring, and I feel the moment right before he falls over the edge. His hips stutter, breath catching, shaft throbbing against my palm—

Then the click of a gun being readied echoes through the room like a death toll.

"Well, shit," comes a mocking voice from the doorway. "You two started without me."

Charon moves so fast I barely register it, whipping around to shield me with his body.

Jonas just laughs, stepping inside with a pistol trained at our heads. "Ah, ah. Don't bother. You wouldn't get far before I put a hole in your freaky little head." His eye flicks to me with a sickening gleam that makes my stomach churn. "You see, I called dibs on that one, and I've come to claim my prize. Miss me, sweetheart?"

CHAPTER TWENTY-FIVE

Charon

Nyx launches from the window, talons aimed for Jonas's other eye, but he sidesteps at the last minute.

"Not this time, birdie."

She sails through the open door into the hallway, which he quickly closes, locking her out.

I lunge while his back is turned, slamming into his shoulder. The gun fires once, but the bullet goes wide, shattering the window as we crash into the wall. Hector shouts when Jonas's elbow connects with my nose, hard enough to daze me.

He's stronger than he looks, fingers clawing at my face as I try to wrestle the gun from his grip. We stumble over a chair, and I use the weight of it to throw him off-balance, sending us both to the floor in a tangle of limbs and snarling teeth.

A headbutt sends blood spurting from my already aching nose, but I manage to knock the pistol loose. It skids across the room, where Hector dives for it.

"I don't think so," Jonas grunts, driving a knee into my chest before launching himself toward Hector instead.

No.

I grab his ankle, wrenching it backward with all the strength I have left. There's a sickening pop as he crashes down, screaming, but not before he wraps his arms around Hector's thighs and pulls him to the ground, too.

My heart drops completely when he rolls over onto his back, gun in hand, the barrel shoved against Hector's temple with an arm binding his chest.

Time slows. The room tilts under my feet, silent except for the rasp of Jonas's breath and my blood roaring in my ears.

Hector doesn't scream. He just looks up at me with wide, terrified eyes, and that fear makes me see red.

"On your knees, freak," Jonas grins through blood-streaked teeth, "or I'll paint this floor with his brains."

My vision swims from the blow to my head as I whisper the words, *"You don't want to do this."*

He sneers, moving the gun to Hector's jaw. "Wrong. I've wanted to do this since the fucking boat."

The barrel presses so hard into Hector's skin that it leaves a mark. One wrong move from me, and Jonas pulls the trigger, ending everything I fought for tonight in a spray of blood I'll never scrub from my soul.

So I kneel slowly, lifting my hands into the air as my lungs struggle to work.

"Good choice." Jonas laughs harshly against Hector's neck. "Would've been a shame to mess up this pretty face."

Hector's chest heaves under Jonas's arm, but he keeps his gaze on mine.

"Please," I whisper, the shape of the word burning my throat like acid.

Jonas only tightens his grip as he gets to his knees, shoving Hector to the ground face-first. "Here's what's gonna happen. I'm going to fuck your rotter so hard he passes out, and you're gonna sit there and watch. Then we'll see who's still alive out in the pit for a turn, how about that?"

"Don't!" Hector shouts, struggling to get free, but Jonas presses the gun to the back of his head.

I shift up in fear, just a fraction, but Jonas clocks it.

"I said *sit the fuck down!*" he growls, dragging Hector upright like a human shield.

My body trembles with the effort it takes to hold back.

I could end this. I could leap over, tackle him, rip him apart, but if I'm too slow... if I'm off by a second—

"Why are you doing this?" Hector asks, fingers fighting to pry Jonas's arm from his chest. "You already lost. Lena is dead. What's even the point?"

"Dead?" Jonas laughs sharply, empty socket pulsing with fury. "You think this ends just because she's gone? Oh, no, sweetheart. She might have thought she was in charge, but I was always calling the shots. I'm the Judge now."

Hector snarls angrily. "Then *do it*. Pull the trigger and kill us both, you fucking coward."

My breath catches in my throat.

"Not before I've had my fun." He shoves Hector down again, moving the gun away from his face as both hands yank down Hector's pants, and my body snaps into motion before I can blink.

My shoulder slams into his ribs with a *crunch*, knocking him to the ground. Hector shouts, scrambling backward as I pin Jonas beneath me and slam his hand down until the pistol skitters away.

He swings blindly, teeth bared, but I catch his wrist in midair and twist sharply, snapping it under my grip.

"I'll fucking kill you, freak!" Jonas snarls, but I drive my fist into his face once, twice, six times, bashing his forehead in.

Freak. How many times has he spat that word at me over the years? How many times has he treated me like a *fucking* animal?!

Grabbing his cheeks, I shove my fingers into his mouth and wrap them around his bottom teeth. He starts to buck beneath me, thrashing in fury, but I've got him pinned. Using all of my strength, I yank down, pulling and pulling until skin starts to tear.

Jonas lets out a bloody scream when his jawbone snaps, coming clean off in my hand. Just as I go to force it down his throat, Hector's touch on my bicep stops me cold.

"Wait."

I freeze, panting, blood dripping from my knuckles. Jonas gurgles beneath me, his mutilated face no longer human.

"Charon." Hector's voice is soft in my ear. "Don't kill him. Not yet."

My gaze stays on the man beneath me, the monster who almost took everything from me. Who hurt him. Hurt what's *mine*.

But Hector's hand stays firm on my arm, his lips caressing my neck. So I unclench my fist slowly, letting the jawbone drop to the floor.

"Good. That's good. Now look at me."

My eyes swing to him, to the gun in his hand now aimed at the wheezing creature beneath me. Fire burns in his eyes as he stares back, but it's not anger. It's something deeper, something *raw*. His hand finds my cheek as he closes the distance between us and crushes his mouth to mine.

The kiss is warm, insistent, and I meet him with everything I have—all the fear, the ache, the need. I grip his waist, pulling him closer, gasping against his lips when he sucks my bottom one between his teeth.

A soft, desperate noise escapes him, one that'll haunt me forever as he delves his fingers into my hair, tugging hard.

"I want to belong to you," he says, pulling back to inhale deeply before reaching for my zipper, gun still trained on Jonas. "Please. Show him who I belong to."

CHAPTER TWENTY-SIX

Hector

Possessive desire swells within me, sharp and all-consuming.

Charon's hands move automatically, sliding under my shirt to feel the heat of my skin. I want to mark him with something no one—not even death—can take from me. I want to drown in him, make him forget the horrors, the pain, the man dying beneath us.

"Mine," he whispers against my neck, dragging his teeth along my pulse point.

With a shudder, I tip my head back and reach inside his pants to pull out his heavy length. "Yes. Gods, yes."

My hand strokes him faster as he thrusts against my palm desperately, sucking on my throat hard enough to break skin, like every part of him needs to live inside me.

When warmth trickles down my throat, I moan, letting go of him to swipe a hand through the bite. Crimson stains my fingers, and I wrap them around his cock again, spreading my blood over his shaft. "Lean back."

Obeying my command, Charon lowers himself over Jonas's legs, whose rattling breaths fill the room. I use his shoulders to stand, body trembling as I undo my trousers before dropping them to the floor. When my length juts upward, he dips his head to lick along my glistening tip, pulling a hiss of pleasure from my throat.

"Bite me again," I murmur, straddling his lap to sit on his thighs. He releases a sharp breath as our shafts glide together. "Make me bleed. I want to carry your mark into the afterlife when I go."

A growl rumbles deep in his chest as he grabs my hips, holding me in place. My pulse thrums beneath my skin, begging to be claimed, and something primal in the Ferryman answers. He leans forward, dragging his lips over the shell of my ear before mouthing, *"You're not going anywhere without me."*

Then he sinks his teeth into the juncture between my neck and shoulder, deep enough to scar.

I cry out, my whole body arching as warm metallic rolls down my skin. With the gun still pointed at Jonas, I wrap my free hand around our lengths and stroke roughly, neither of us caring when the body beneath starts to spasm.

"Kiss me," I moan, my hips jerking against his hold.

He takes my lips again, and my tongue laps into his mouth, gathering saliva and blood. Pulling away, I gaze down at my fist as I part my jaw, letting red-tinted spit drip onto our cocks. It mixes with the precum leaking from us both, and each slick pass of my palm pulls a shaky breath out of Charon.

But it's not enough.

"I need..." Biting my bottom lip, I look up at him from under my lashes in shame. "I want more, but I don't...know how. If I can. What those soldiers did to me when I was young..."

Fury and vengeance flash in his eyes, pupils completely blown out. He softens his grip, letting go of my hips to cradle my face with a slow shake of his head. *No. Not shame. Never.*

"I'm sorry," I whisper brokenly.

Charon reaches for my hand, the one still holding the gun, before guiding the barrel until it rests against his chest—right over his heart.

My eyes go wide, heart slamming into my ribs. "Charon—"

He shakes his head again, covering my hand with his as he pours every word he's trying to say into his gaze. Leaning in, he kisses my forehead, then my cheek, moving to my lips where he mouths the words, *"You're in control."*

My jaw quivers, fingers tightening on the grip of the gun. Moisture pools on my tongue, and I spit onto his length one more time before rising onto my knees.

"I don't want to hurt you," I sob, dropping down just slightly enough that the tip of his cock rests against my hole.

That only makes him smile. *You won't.*

He doesn't need to mouth the words. I can see them in his eyes, in the way he leans back just enough to let me take this at my own pace. His hands stay low on my thighs, thumbs brushing steady circles into my skin.

My breath catches when I lower myself just a little more, pain and pleasure warring within. The burn is fleeting thanks to these rotter genes, but...I like it. Because I'm with *him*. My legs start to tremble when my body resists and relents all at once.

"You're safe," he mouths against my cheek. *"I've got you."*

My ass eventually settles against his thighs as my hole swallows his cock tightly. Charon seems to be forcing himself still, and I release a breathy moan, letting myself adjust. When I finally start to move with slow, shallow rolls of my hips, it's not about pleasure, not at first. It feels like reclaiming what was taken from me.

Our rhythm stutters and shakes, but I keep going, my knuckles white on the gun. Tears burn hot at the corners of my eyes, but he kisses them away. His fingertips trail up my spine as I shudder with every inch I take back for myself.

"You're okay," he mouths, even though he knows I'm not. Maybe we both never will be. *"You're mine."*

I grind down harder, the drag of his cock inside me sparking a cry of pleasure, and I can see his self-control starting to fray.

"I need more," I choke out, rising up to slam back down again, my length dripping between us. "Please. Make me feel you."

Gripping my hips tight, Charon helps guide my movements as I start to ride him hard. His fingers thread through my curls, tugging lightly to raise my gaze. Those blue eyes lock on mine, wild and dark and *begging*. I rock faster, the slap of skin drowning out the gurgles of a dying man.

"Mine," I hiss, burying my face in his shoulder. "You're fucking *mine*."

He endures it all for me—my teeth at his throat, the barrel of the gun bruising his chest, my hole choking his cock like I never want to let go. Tilting his head, he bares his neck as if daring me to take more. To claim him as he's claimed me.

My teeth sink in deep, leaving a mark that'll outlast whatever hell still waits for us outside this room.

Fire explodes behind his eyes as he holds my hips still, fucking up into me with a rolling growl. I cry out, reaching between us to stroke myself hard, my entire body bowing with ecstasy when the orgasm takes control. I come with his name on my tongue, painting both our stomachs in cum before I whip the gun towards Jonas's head and pull the trigger.

Blood sprays Charon's cheek, but he keeps thrusting, too far lost in the pleasure to care.

When he finally spills inside me, it's with his teeth buried in my throat. I collapse against him, sweaty and panting, heartbeat hammering like a war drum. He wraps his arms around me tightly when the pistol clatters to the ground, gunshot still echoing off the walls.

And even though we're still trapped inside this prison, with monsters and mayhem waiting for us beyond these walls, I've never felt more free.

CHAPTER TWENTY-SEVEN

Charon's heartbeat thumps steadily beneath my ears.

Cold air from the shattered window cools the sweat and blood on my skin, my hole aching from his cock still buried inside me. It twitches as I shift, turning my head to gaze up at him.

His eyes meet mine, blue as deep as twilight, wrinkling at the corners when he smiles at me.

In that smile, I find my undoing. More so than what we just did, or the man I just killed. There's no pity in it, no malice. No fear. He looks at me like I'm something precious.

My fingers curl against his bicep as I breathe him in, trying to memorize his warmth, the comforting rhythm of his pulse, the way his breath hitches when I press my lips to his sternum.

"Thank you for showing me how to live," I murmur.

Charon's brow furrows as he mouths something I can't hear before kissing my temple lightly, so damn soft that tears sting behind my lashes again. How can he be this way? After everything he's been through, everything that happened tonight, how can he still be so gentle when the world has hurt him over and over?

Maybe someday, he'll teach me. If we survive the night.

As if on cue, a groan rattles through the air, followed by the wet smack of something heavy hitting the door.

Charon tenses beneath me.

I turn around just as another body slams into the wood, harder this time. And then another. The hinges start to creak.

Our time is up.

He eases me off his lap, cock slipping free as I force my legs to cooperate. My body protests, but I move anyway, pulling on my clothes because survival demands it.

The shattered window still gapes, glass blown out, jagged teeth glinting in the dark. Beyond, a red moon sparks off the water, and a shudder wracks my frame at the thought of plunging into those dark depths.

"We have no other choice, do we?" I rasp, flinching when another biter slams into the door, no doubt drawn by the sound of my gunshot.

Charon climbs through first without hesitation, carefully avoiding sharp shards before turning to offer me his hand.

I step back instead, heart pounding as I stare at the black waves below, churning with something unnatural. Another bang rocks the door behind me, wood screaming as it splinters.

"*Hector*." Charon's voice is only a whisper, his hand still outstretched, blue eyes wide and pleading.

I know I should reach for him. I want to trust the fall, but I swear something's moving in that water. It smells like rust and decay. There *has* to be another way. The roof, or maybe another room? Maybe we could fight our way out—

Before I can deliberate too long, the door explodes inward, making me jump. The first biter barrels through, half its face hanging by sinew, a gurgling screech tearing from its throat. Others follow, pouring into the room like a flood of nightmares.

Charon grabs me from behind, wrapping his arms around my waist.

"Wait—" I start to shout, but he hauls me through the window just as something grazes my leg.

It takes me far too long to realize that we're falling. A scream tears from my throat, the night air whipping past as the world disappears in a blur of rising water.

The cold swallows us whole on impact, filling my nostrils and lungs with a bitter liquid that chokes me down. The current rips me from Charon's arms as I spin into the torrent.

My ears ring with the silence of pressure. Something brushes my ankle, and I kick out, heart lurching when my leg clips debris, dislodging the rifle. Everything burns. My lungs scream for air.

Forcing my eyes open, I spot a shimmer of light above, slicing through the murk. I swim toward it mindlessly, clawing with heavy muscles. My fingers break the surface first, then my mouth. Air rushes in, flooding my senses with dizzying relief.

"Charon!" I cough, blinking away the water's sting.

There's no answer, just the sound of fire crackling in the distance and the splashes of biters following us out the window.

"Charon, where are you?"

Still, nothing other than the snarls and howls closing in fast.

Panic claws at my chest. I spin again, treading water frantically.

We went under at the same time. He should've surfaced by now.

Why hasn't he surfaced?

"Charon!" My voice breaks, swallowed by the night.

A piercing caw answers back from above as a shadow cuts through the rising smoke.

"Nyx?"

She circles twice, then dives low, shrieking with urgency before veering off toward the east bank. My gut twists as I force my body to follow, teeth chattering. Every inch feels like a mile. The water thickens with filth and blood, the growls behind me growing louder.

Finally, a figure comes into focus;

Charon, floating face down against a half-submerged plank of wood.

"*No*," I breathe, surging forward to grab the back of his shirt and haul him upright. His head lolls to the side, eyes closed...but he's breathing. It's shallow and strained, but it's there, puffing in a cloud around his face. Fresh blood pours from a wound across his cheek.

"You stubborn asshole." Wrapping my arm around his chest to keep him above water, I glance up at Nyx to lead the way again. Where, I've no idea, but I follow her with everything I have left because anywhere's better than this river teeming with biters.

The shore is still far, the night is still hungry, and neither of us is safe yet.

Charon feels like dead weight in my arms.

Every stroke toward shore is a battle, my limbs screaming. He's too heavy against the current, but I push through the exhaustion, unwilling to let him go. Not when his heart is still beating against my ribs.

The water thickens with sludge the closer we get to land. Something oily and foul slicks past my leg, and I gag, swallowing another mouthful of filth. Behind us, the slap of rotted limbs splashing into the water moves closer.

"Come on," I grit, tightening my grip on Charon's chest. "Just a little further."

Nyx screeches again, wings slicing the air as she banks sharply, disappearing into the mist. I want to scream after her, beg her not to leave us behind, but when I look up again, I see it.

Land.

A broken dock, half-sunken, the warped wood groaning under the lapping tide. Beyond it, a cracked tower rises tall on a distant bluff, half-swallowed by vines. I recognize it from old photographs Father used to show me. A lighthouse, some relic from old times that used to guide ships to shore. The river's current must have pulled us closer to the sea.

My foot finds the riverbed first, slipping in the muck. I use the last of my strength to drag us forward, inch by agonizing inch, until we collapse onto the bank in a heap. Storm clouds thunder above the mist, dark and slightly tinged with crimson, a warning of red rain approaching. My chest tightens anxiously at the thought of getting caught in a downpour.

Rolling Charon onto his side, I slap at his back roughly, hoping to dislodge whatever might have gotten into his lungs. He jerks suddenly, convulsing as murky water erupts from his mouth in a choking gasp, coughing so hard his whole body shakes.

"Breathe. It's okay, get it all out."

Another violent cough leaves his throat, then another, until finally his breath steadies into shallow pants. His hand scrapes weakly against the mud, fingers curling toward mine when his eyes crack open beneath swollen lids. He's ghostly pale, his lips tinged purple, but he's *breathing*.

"We made it," I whisper, cradling his face. "Charon, we *fucking made it.*"

His lips move, but I miss what he mouths when lightning cracks open the sky—electricity skitters across my skin, corrosive and toxic. Rain isn't far behind.

My eyes swing toward the lighthouse cutting through the fog on the hill. "We have to move."

Pressing a quick kiss to his temple, I clench my teeth and let him lift me up. With his arm slung across my shoulders, we begin the climb, both of us using each other for leverage. Mud sucks at my boot, the weight of him dragging me down. Charon's head rolls against my shoulder, but somehow he helps me up the winding slope.

"Almost there," I grunt, shaking from the cold.

Lightning strikes again, illuminating the lighthouse like a ghost, its paint stripped and glass shattered. By the time we reach the gaping entrance, my muscles scream from exhaustion. I shoulder through right after Nyx with a snarl, falling into the dark just as the first drops of rain come crashing down.

Charon immediately collapses, taking me with him. We hit the floor *hard*, and I land on his heaving chest, my heart hammering in my ears. His eyes flutter open, only for a second, blood still leaking from the cut on his cheek.

"We're here," I croak, gripping his arms as spots begin to dance in my vision. "You're safe. I've got you."

A hint of a smile pulls at his mouth before he slips back into unconsciousness. Lightning strikes once more, illuminating his face, and it's the last thing I see before darkness also takes me, too.

CHAPTER TWENTY-EIGHT

Two days pass and the rain doesn't let up.

Charon drifts between consciousness, shivers wracking his body from fever. All I can do is slump against the wall with his head on my lap and wait for the storm to pass.

There's no food here, no dry clothes. Just the sound of the rain pummeling the lighthouse and Nyx's feathers ruffling whenever the lightning hits too close. My stomach growls hungrily.

When was the last time I ate something? Days ago? I can't even remember. All I know is the frenzy hasn't hit, for one reason or another, and I'm not questioning it. Maybe my body is just too malnourished to react.

Around us, the wind blows in from cracks in the foundation. Water leaks from up above, forming a pool of red near the far side of the circular space. A spiral staircase that once led to the top now sits rusted through, steps broken and crumbling.

Old, moldy crates pile in one corner. I'd hoped they might hold supplies when I checked earlier, but they were empty, just nests of long-decayed rodents. Whatever this place must have been was abandoned long ago.

Nyx lands near the entrance, cawing low before hopping away into the shadows, probably feeling cooped up.

I run a hand over Charon's damp strands, brushing them away from his face. He'd gotten sick last night, vomiting up more river muck, and it's only getting worse. His skin is too warm, breath too shallow. He needs something to drink and medicine. Probably food, too.

I don't know what the fuck to do.

If I could go back to Aster's Hollow, I would. Try to find rations, bring them here. But I have no idea how far we've drifted—if it's a mile or fifty. Hiking there could take days, and I've only got one foot. Charon doesn't have days. What if I turn while he's passed out and he can't fight me off? What if I kill him? I'd rather die.

"Charon," I whisper, pulling him closer. Tears sting my eyes. "I don't know how to help you."

We're trapped, and it's probably all my fault. If I had just let him end Jonas instead of wanting the kill for myself, we would have had time to think of a plan, some other escape besides the raging river. But I was *selfish*. I wanted retribution, and I wanted Charon. Somehow, those two goals became entangled in my head until I couldn't have one without the other. Now look where we ended up.

A scuffle in the dark catches my attention, sending my heart racing. My grip tightens, every muscle locked for a fight, but a disgruntled caw stirs the air.

Nyx swoops out of the shadows, something caught in her talons. She drops it on the floor beside me before landing a few feet away, head cocked in my direction.

I gaze down at it, my cracked lips curling in disgust. "That's...a dead rat."

She clicks her beak, nudging the vermin toward me. *"Good to go."*

"Nyx, we can't eat a rat. It's infected—" I cut myself off, a flare of anger slicing through me at the memory of Lena's lies. "It probably has all kinds of diseases." Well. Not that I suppose it would matter, with my rotter immune system. But for Charon, it would. "It's filthy."

She caws angrily, kicking the thing before taking off toward the wooden crates in a flurry of feathers.

"I looked in those already, there's *nothing*. We have no food, no water, no fucking *fire*—"

Once again, I stop mid-sentence when my gaze drops to the crate she's dancing on, the one made of decaying wood.

Wood that can *burn*.

Hope blooms in my chest.

I slide Charon off my lap and lower him gently to the ground, brushing his matted strands away from his fevered brow. "Hold on, okay? I'll make it better."

Nyx flutters aside when I step closer to prying up every dry shard of wood I can find. Bits of packing straw cling to the bottom, too, maybe enough to use as kindling. I pile what I can salvage in the middle of the floor.

It should all work fine, but...how to ignite it?

Searching the edges of the room, I look for something to use as a flint. Old bits of metal piping catch my eye, along with a rock just jagged enough to spark. There's no guarantee I'll be able to get a fire going, but at this point, I'll try anything.

Whatever I can do to see that smile on Charon's face again.

Kneeling on the cracked floor, I press some straw between two thin slats and start striking with my rock once, twice. Ten times.

A ragged breath punches out of me, sweat mixing with the grime and river filth clinging to my skin. My palms begin to bleed as I try over, and over, and *over*—

Finally, something sparks.

But dies instantly.

Gritting my teeth, I try again, hunching over like a fucking cave dweller. Another spark ignites, followed by a twitch of smoke.

"Come on, come on," I whisper through my teeth, begging the gods or the universe or whatever is listening as I strike again.

The smoke grows, straw hissing with a crackle, and then...blessedly, a flame.

I almost snuff it out when a relieved laugh leaves my lungs, curling my body around the warmth to feed it slivers of wood. The fire grows brighter.

Behind me, Charon shifts, letting out a quiet breath. I turn toward him just long enough to whisper, "I got you, baby. Just hang on."

The rat comes next. I skewer it with a piece of rusted metal, gagging slightly as I hold it over the flames.

Nyx flutters down from wherever she was perched, landing beside me. "*Good to go.*"

I just nod, too tired to respond.

The flames dance in the gloom, casting wild shadows on the crumbling walls. I turn the meat slowly while wincing at the sound of sizzling fur. It smells vile, but it's food. We don't have the luxury of being picky.

When the thing looks less...disgusting, I tear it in two with my fingers and scarf down my half without thought, no time for gagging. My body needs it.

Charon moves again, and I crawl the short distance between us. "Hey."

His skin's still too warm, cheeks flushed in a way that has nothing to do with the fire. But his eyes crack open just enough for me to catch a glint of recognition.

"You with me?" I ask, touching his forehead.

He blinks once.

"I made a fire. Cooked you a rat and everything." A ghost of a smile tugs at the corner of his mouth, cracking my heart in two as I press the meat to his lips. "Eat. Just a little, okay?"

It takes a second, but then his mouth parts, and I ease the bite inside. He chews agonizingly slow, but he does it, swallowing hard when he's finished.

"That's it," I breathe, brushing a kiss over his cheek. "I'll figure out how to boil us some water next."

Nyx flutters up onto another crate and tucks her beak under her wing, content for now. The rain keeps pounding against the lighthouse above, that pool of red water on the floor growing darker. But Charon is still breathing. His fingers curl around my leg as I feed him small bites at a time, planting kisses all over his face. Later, I'll explore more of this place when he's fed.

For now, we're still here. Surviving.

That's all the hope I can afford.

CHAPTER TWENTY-NINE

Charon

Complete silence draws me from sleep.

Soft, unfamiliar stillness. No thunder, no screaming wind. Just birdsong and the lapping ocean waves. For the first time in what feels like days, I don't ache like I'm dying.

My eyes blink open slowly, the hazy gold of morning light spilling through cracks in the lighthouse walls. Warmth caresses my skin, not fever-warmth, but...sunlight.

Shifting slightly on the ground, I test my limbs. They're still sore and weak, but I'm not shaking or burning like I was when Hector fed me—

Hector.

I bolt straight up, too fast, black dots dancing at the edge of my sight. A blanket slips from my shoulders when I take in the pile of burnt ashes in the center of the room, flames long since dead.

He's not here.

Panic claws at my chest as I stand, my knees nearly buckling. Steadying myself against the stone wall, I listen for any signs of him with spasming lungs.

Once the rush of blood in my ears dissipates, I finally hear his muffled voice—a murmur of words I can't quite dissect, followed by a sharp little squawk from Nyx. I follow the sound down a vine-covered hallway until I spot the edge of a trapdoor tucked behind a broken crate. Faint light filters up from below.

"...we're saving these for him," Hector chastises, clicking his tongue. "You're such a little shit."

Nyx caws in protest.

I descend the stairs carefully, clinging to the rail as each step groans beneath my weight. At the bottom, I pause, taking in what seems like some kind of cellar. It's warmer than upstairs, tucked away from the wind. Stone walls curve in a half-circle, stacked with rusted shelves covered in jars and cans of...*food*. A small bed sits in the far corner, blankets tossed aside, and old photographs line the wall beside it.

Hector sits cross-legged on the floor with a jar between his knees and Nyx perched on one shoulder. Tongue caught between his teeth, blond curls an adorable mess, skin clean as if he some-how scrubbed away the last few days.

He looks up when I reach the last step, relief flooding his fea-tures. "Hey. You're awake."

I nod as Nyx launches from his shoulder, fluttering to mine. She nips at my jaw affectionately, and I run a finger down her beak, gaze still on Hector.

"You look better," he adds, emerald eyes roaming my frame. "Still pale, but not as bad."

Using a shelf for leverage, he pulls himself up before hopping over to me. His hand hovers uncertainly in the air, like he's unsure whether to touch me or not, so I pull him into my arms and place a soft kiss on his lips. Nyx smacks my cheek with her wing as she flutters away in annoyance, but Hector sighs into my mouth, melting against my chest.

"I was worried you wouldn't make it," he rasps, stealing another kiss before gesturing to the covered shelves. "But look, look what I found. There's stuff to eat, and medicine. At least...I assumed it was medicine when I gave it to you. There was a giant red cross on it. And I boiled us some rainwater. If I'd known all this stuff was down here a few days ago, I, uh...wouldn't have fed you a dead rat."

My lips twitch as I squeeze him, attention drifting to the yellowed photos near the bed. Snapshots of lives long gone—a young couple smiling in front of the lighthouse, one of a picnic spread across a blanket with silver glinting in the sky. Smiling, sun-kissed faces.

Hector follows my stare. "I don't know who this place belonged to, but I think they're dead."

I nod once, brushing my thumb gently over the back of his neck. We stand like that for a moment, swaying slightly in the quiet cellar, letting the silence stretch between us as we study the photos. A ghost of laughter clings to the images, like a life paused mid-breath.

"I was thinking we could stay," he murmurs eventually, gazing up at me. "I mean, there's a bed now. A real one. Maybe we could learn to fish or hunt. I know they used to do that back at Aster's Hollow, but the Judge put a stop to it when I was young—"

He cuts himself off with a wince, and I reach out, tucking a strand of hair behind his ear. My fingers linger along his jaw until he leans into my palm with a breathy little laugh, the first I've ever heard him make. It's beautiful. I could spend the rest of my life pulling that sound out of him.

"You think we could do it?" he asks after a beat, grasping my wrist. "Build something here? Just...exist, you and me?" An irritated caw echoes from the corner. "And your murder bird."

I wish I could shout *'yes'* out loud, wish I had the words he deserves to hear. But instead, I press my forehead to his, closing my eyes as I let my answer bleed into my touch, into the way I hold him like he's the most precious thing in the world to me.

Opening my eyes, I glance one last time at the photographs, wondering what kind of love the couple in them shared, what held them together when the world fell apart. Was it as fierce as what I feel for Hector? Did they get to keep it until the very end?

I hope so.

Maybe if we're careful, if we're lucky, we'll last long enough to be like the people in those photos, too.

"I love you," I whisper against his ear, savoring the slight noise that comes from his throat.

His fingers thread into my hair, and when he kisses me again, it's slow and sure like a promise.

For once, I believe we might just get to keep this, even if the world still burns around us. I know we still have things to do, like finding my boat and my mother's book, maybe looting what's left of Zone T for supplies before anyone else does.

But all of that can wait.

Because we're both here, our hearts are still beating, and I don't want to waste another breath living in the past.

CHAPTER THIRTY

Hector

"Who do you think they were?"

Charon shifts behind me, his chest pressed to my spine as his arm loops tighter around my waist.

I tilt my head, studying the pictures on the wall next to us. The people in them smile brightly, as if they didn't know the world was ending. One shows a couple swimming in the ocean, while another has them standing on the dock in fancy clothes.

"Family, maybe," I muse, running my thumb over their faces. "They look happy. Or, at least, pretending to be. Guess that's all any of us ever do."

His lips press between my shoulder blades in silent agreement, and for a moment, I pretend that picture-perfect kind of life was never out of reach. That maybe, here in this lighthouse, it belonged to us all along.

Swallowing hard, I lean back when his fingertips graze my ribs. He just finished using the water I'd boiled to wash up while I got us some food. The trap door is shut, Nyx keeping watch from her perch on a shelf across the room. For the first time in years, I feel...safe. Fed.

I swing my gaze over to the empty jars on the floor. "Can't believe we had peaches. I haven't had them since I was ten, and they weren't even moldy."

Charon huffs softly, nose bumping my ear. His hand anchors me in place, rubbing lazy circles that send goosebumps across my flesh.

"Never thought I'd feel full again, either," I say, taking his hand to press it flat against my chest. "Not just in my stomach, but *here*, too."

His thumb brushes my nipple in response, sending tingles down to my toes. When his other hand moves lower, sweeping the skin just under my naval, my cock twitches at the touch.

One day, Charon and I will be just like the people in the photos, our faces and story long lost to this world.

But not tonight. Not yet.

A slight moan leaves my throat when he kisses the back of my neck, his stiff length pressing into my back. He's been hard for hours, but he hasn't taken things further yet. I think he's waiting for permission.

So I give it to him.

Taking his wrist, I move his hand slowly beneath the hem of my pants, sucking in a breath when his fingers wrap around my cock. My hips buck as he strokes me slowly, his nose dragging up the side of my throat before his teeth sink into my skin.

"Yes." A shudder works its way down my spine. "I'm yours. All yours."

Charon growls low. I gasp softly when his other hand explores my nipple, tweaking it gently. Every nerve ending in my body lights up, straining for more.

His pelvis rolls forward, grinding against me in a steady rhythm, and I groan while precum leaks down my shaft. It's not fast or rough like before. Just deliberately patient. We have all the time in the world to go slow.

Our eyes lock when I look at him over my shoulder, catching the awe shining in his gaze.

"I'm yours," I say again, voice shaking. "And you're mine."

He kisses me softly, his arm tightening around my chest to hold me still. The other moves with the rhythm of his strokes, jerking my cock until I'm a squirming mess, greedy for more.

And I do. I *want* more, just...maybe not like before.

What happened between us inside Zone T was beautiful and healing, but I love him just like this—touching me, making me feel alive.

Shoving my pants down, I free my length to give him more access. He cradles my sac tenderly, and I nearly come from the sensation alone.

"Charon." Grabbing his wrist, I push his hand away before turning to face him. He shifts instinctively to make room, and my fingers fumble at the button of his trousers. "I need you to feel this, too. Let me touch you. Please."

He nods, desire etched on his features as his hands fall to his sides, giving me space and trust. My heart stutters when I lower his zipper before reaching in to pull out his length.

He's flushed and leaking, his thick swollen tip making me salivate. My palm runs down the side, and his hips jerk, a soundless gasp leaving his throat. I study his face the entire time, searching for signs of discomfort, but there aren't any. Only *need*.

I go slow at first, kissing a path down his chest until he's panting. His head falls back against the wall when I reach his stomach.

"I want you to feel good," I whisper, settling between his legs. "You deserve that. You deserve everything."

He threads his fingers through my hair, guiding me to his cock without ever taking his eyes off mine. There's something heartbreakingly beautiful in the way he watches me, like he still doesn't understand how I could want him in this way.

I want him in every way possible, for the rest of my life.

His whole body arches once I take him into my mouth, his grip tightening in my hair. I use my tongue to learn what he likes, what makes his breath hitch and his thighs tremble, what has his eyelids drooping in ecstasy. I've never done this before, but the salty taste of his cum and the way he never drops his gaze are intoxicating.

Charon may be quiet, but his body sings for me.

When he finally comes, I swallow him down, shivering at the way he slides his palm to my throat to feel my muscles flex. Something primal darkens in his expression, a deep growl vibrating his body. As soon as his cock stops pulsing, he reaches down to haul me up onto his chest, causing me to brace my palms against the wall with a yelp.

"Charon, what are you—"

He dives for my cock instantly, wrapping large hands around my waist to scoot me toward his shoulders. A strangled cry leaves my lungs when he closes his lips around my aching shaft, sucking me all the way in until my sac hits his chin.

"Oh, fuck," I breathe, tangling my fingers into his silky strands as I meet his darkened gaze. He tightens his grip on me, pushing me back only to yank me forward again, maneuvering my body so that I'm thrusting into his mouth.

It feels so good that my eyes nearly roll back, but I force them to stay on his face. Saliva slicks my dick, leaking from the corners of his lips when he takes me as deep as he can. Every muscle tenses, my stomach clenching at my impending release.

"C-Charon, I'm...I'm gonna..."

He picks up the pace, swallowing around my cock in a way that has me whimpering. The moment his fingers slide between my crease, I come with a shout, throwing my head back as I unload into his throat. He holds me through it, massaging the fleshy part of my ass with his palms while he drinks me down.

My arms and legs give out once I finish, and I slip from his mouth, dropping breathlessly to the mattress beside him. His strong arms gather me up as he buries his face in my hair, a contented sigh leaving his lips. It makes me chuckle into his shoulder.

"I...that was..." Shaking my head, I lift my gaze to his, finding that smile already aimed at me. My heart skips several beats. "Thank you."

His smile deepens, and he brushes his thumb along my jaw like he can't believe I'm real. I don't think I'll ever get used to that look on his face—the way he sees me.

But I hope it never stops.

Pressing a lazy kiss to the corner of his mouth, I hum when he chases it for another. Our lips meet softly as I melt into him completely, the world narrowing down to this one single perfect moment.

"You make me feel safe," I admit, tucking my head beneath his chin. "I don't think I've ever had that before."

Charon kisses the top of my head before resting his cheek there, our breaths syncing like we were made to fit together. Maybe we were. Someone, somewhere, designed Charon just for me, and I for him. I believe that with my whole heart. Two broken souls who went through hell to find each other.

In this cellar, the world is finally calm. Ocean waves lap against the cliff outside as Nyx rustles her wings. Charon's heart beats steadily against my cheek, the quiet sound of his breath a perfect lullaby. It feels like we're right where we need to be.

"Don't float away," I murmur sleepily, pressing one last kiss to his collarbone before letting my eyes fall closed.

His arms stay wrapped around me the entire night.

CHAPTER THIRTY-ONE

Charon

The sun has barely crested the hills, spilling gold over the treetops, when we leave the lighthouse come morning. Damp earth crunches beneath my feet as Hector walks beside me, one hand on his belt to keep his pants up while the other clutches a stick we'd found in the woods earlier. His leg still drags now and then, and it makes my chest ache, watching him stumble over roots and rocks. Every time I glance over, though, he just gives me this lopsided smile that cracks my heart in two. I'll make him a proper walking device when we get home.

Home.

That word sounds foreign in my head.

I'd never imagined it could apply to anything but solitude and silence. The deck of a boat, the echo of my own breath. Sure, there was Nyx when she saw fit to grace me with her presence, but still...it was lonely.

Now, home has a heartbeat. A laugh, a sharp tongue, and the most beautiful eyes I've ever seen.

Hector is *home*.

Last night, I'd gotten the deepest sleep I've ever had in my life. We'd clung to each other through the darkness, waking slowly before the sun had even risen. Both our cocks had already been hard, rubbing together as we kissed lazily, and it didn't take long before we were coming all over ourselves again. If I'd died right at that moment, I would have crossed over a happy man.

"Do you think it's still there?" Hector asks, squinting out into the morning mist clinging to the trees. "Someone could have stolen the boat."

Glancing at the way his brows pinch in concern, I bring his palm to my lips. *"Still there."*

"Yeah? You really think so?"

I nod, not because I know for sure, but because I need to believe it myself.

My fingers twitch just thinking about my mother's book, the pages creased with memory, a bright light that kept me anchored during my father's cruelty. During Lena's experiments.

It's not about sentiment as much as it is proof that something *mattered*. That a world once existed beyond the blood and pain. If someone took the only piece of the past I ever gave a damn about...

Well, we'll figure it out.

Hector takes a deep, shaky breath. "Guess we'll find out soon enough."

Zone T is a day's hike on foot, and the path is risky at best, especially with him ambling. He hadn't argued when I'd whispered where I wanted to go, only started tying the blanket currently slung over my shoulder into a makeshift pack to hold supplies.

Now, with the fog curling low and Nyx circling above, I watch him take each step with a quiet determination that makes me wish I could carry him on my back. I'd tried earlier, but he'd snarled at me.

The sun filters through the trees in broken gold, setting his curls alight, and I have to tear my gaze away before I trip over a rock. He doesn't complain once the longer we walk, even when he stumbles or his breath turns shallow. I think he's afraid I'll tell him to turn around, but I won't. He deserves to prove himself just as much as anyone else.

We're heading back into the belly of the beast, but we're no longer the same men who fled it.

Not anymore.

We reach the top of the waterfall just after sunset.

The cliff juts above the cove, and below, the water glitters in shades of crimson gray. A rusted, paint-covered sign nailed to a tree reads:

WARNING! CONTAMINATED SHORELINE BELOW. DO NOT DRINK. DO NOT SWIM.

Lena's deception, still clinging to the world. I want to rip it down and burn it, but instead, I pass by, guiding Hector over a patch of loose gravel.

His hand brushes mine as he pulls me to a stop. "Is it okay if we rest here for a bit?"

I nod, tightening my grip on his fingers before easing us down onto a slab of stone. He leans against my shoulder, chest heaving and curls damp with sweat. The hike has been more challenging for him than he wants to admit. I had to force him to take breaks.

While his head rests against me, we stare out past the trees where the mist parts, revealing Zone T's watchtowers in the distance. They're still miles off, tall and skeletal, clawing at the sky. How many times did I watch them from the falls below, filling barrel after barrel and wishing I could see them topple over?

But still, they stand, and so do all the lies.

An angry breath leaves my nostrils as I trace the edges of the sign with my gaze, jaw clenching.

"You okay?" Hector's hand trails over my knee.

I start to nod, but shake my head before pointing at the sign.

He follows my finger, head tilting slightly. "I've seen those all over Aster's Hollow. Can't read them, but I know they warn about the water."

Rising to my feet, I reach for it, nails biting into the rotting edge as I rip it from the bark and point to the words bitterly.

Hector watches me carefully. "Lena made them, didn't she?"

All I can do is nod. *That's all I ever do.*

"She wanted people afraid so they'd need her. Obey her." He takes the sign from my hands to stare down at it. "She really made people think the infection was in everything?"

Another fucking nod.

His fingers find the loop of my pants. "And you couldn't tell anyone otherwise."

I look away, throat tightening as I open my mouth, then close it when only a painful whisper comes out. Tapping my lips, I trace the scar across my throat. It's the closest I can come to explaining what happened.

"She told me about it." Hector's eyes darken with fury. "What she did to your mom. How she...hurt you to keep you quiet."

My lids sink closed, fists clenching at my sides from raw pain that the memory brings.

"She turned you into a monster while she played the savior. But not to me." He pulls himself up, wrapping his arms around me tightly. "I saw you, baby. I *see* you. Just like you saw me."

His breath ghosts over my jaw, and I gently cup the back of his head as I dip down to kiss him hard, clinging to his warmth.

"I see you," he repeats, firmer this time.

We devour each other for a long moment, until my lips start to ache and his shirt soaks through with sweat.

Finally, he pulls back, brushing a strand of hair from his face. "We should keep moving."

Reluctantly, I release him and turn my eyes toward the jagged silhouette of Zone T. Thunder rolls above, the air thickening as if another storm approaches. Our only saving grace is that it won't be red rain, not this time.

Hector stoops to grab his walking stick, casting one last look at the contaminated sign on the ground before kicking it over the edge of the falls. It disappears without making a sound or causing a ripple, taking Lena's memory with it.

"Let's tear the rest down on our way back," he mutters, grabbing my hand.

This time, I nod with conviction, because we *will* come back. With our boat, and my mother's book.

Together.

CHAPTER THIRTY-TWO

Nector

Z one T looks nothing like it did when I first arrived on Charon's boat.

What's left of the compound looms ahead, a blackened skeleton of what it used to be. The towers are still standing, but rubble chokes the outer perimeter, scorched metal and burnt flesh coating my nostrils.

I stumble to a stop, breath catching when my eyes find the boat bobbing gently against the dock, completely unscathed.

"It's still here," I breathe in disbelief.

Charon's gaze scans the vessel before taking in our surroundings.

The closer we get, the more the destruction around us becomes real. Half of the building collapsed, a section of the wall just a heap of concrete and twisted barbed wire. It looks completely dead...but not everything died.

Shadows dart between the ruins, catching my eye. Survivors, maybe. Raiders searching for anything left.

Or maybe something worse.

Gripping Charon's wrist, I gesture toward the boat with a thundering heart. "Quick. Before they spot us."

He scoops me up, cradling my body to his chest as he nearly runs the rest of the way. Whoever used it last left the ramp lowered, but just as we climb aboard, something screams inhumanly behind us.

"Shit, shit," I gasp, gripping the railing when Charon sets me down. "Oh fuck!"

The first biter lurches into view from behind the wall, half its body burned clean off, exposing blackened bone. Then another, and another. Dozens pour out from the guts of Zone T, some of them guards and others prisoners.

Charon yanks the ramp halfway up before the rusted pulley catches, grinding to a halt. He growls angrily, throwing his full weight into it.

"They're coming!"

The dock cracks as the first biter slams into the base of the ramp, snarling up at us with blood-crusted teeth. Charon jerks the mechanism again, hard enough to make the ramp jolt. Finally, *mercifully*, the damn thing clatters into place with a bone-rattling slam.

But the infected aren't giving up.

One of them leaps, arms outstretched. Its fingers claw at the railing as it drags itself upward like a fucking nightmare.

Nyx caws angrily, swooping down from the sky to rake her talons across its face, causing the thing to lose its grip and fall into the water below.

But more keep coming.

I scramble toward the back, ignoring a fleeting throb in my leg as I check the sail's bindings. "Come on, come on."

Charon steps in, dragging the heavy tarp free, and its patched cloth catches the wind, but not fast enough.

"Row!" I scream, fumbling for the thing he uses to steer. "Row, baby, now!"

He's beside me in an instant, directing the boat away from the dock, muscles straining with each pull. The sail fills, lurching us forward just as another biter slams against the hull with a snarl. Clawing fingers swipe at the air behind us, one of them leaping over the railing—

Charon kicks it square in the chest, sending it flying back into the others.

And then we're free, the sail stretching taut overhead as we glide away from the shore.

Biters dive into the water in pursuit, splashing after us, but the current pulls us faster than they can swim. Zone T starts to shrink in the distance, swallowed by night and the howls of the damned.

"Fucking hell." I collapse onto the deck once we're far enough away, my chest heaving in relief. "So much for...grabbing supplies."

He drops down beside me a second later, brows tight with worry and hair a wild mess around his shoulders. The sight sends a carnal zap of lust down my spine, but then his eyes catch on something over my head, and an elated grin spreads across his face.

I follow his gaze curiously, only to choke on my spit when I spot what he's smiling at.

Rations. Bags and bags of rations, piled near the cabin. Crates of silver coins and bullets, too. My lashes flutter as I blink rapidly, certain I've gone mad.

"What the fuck...no. That can't be real." Dragging myself toward the pile, I pull the string on a burlap sack, checking inside. Sure enough, everything is there. Dried meats and fruit, vegetables, bandages. Medicine, too, from what I can see. "This doesn't make any sense."

Charon chuckles as he presses a kiss to my temple, clearly not as shocked as I am. What the hell happened after I left in that water barrel?

Nyx flutters down from above, landing on one of the crates with her chest feathers puffed. *"Good to go."*

I glare at her accusingly. "Did you know about this the entire time?"

She just preens like the little shit that she is.

Charon laughs silently, pulling me closer until I fall into his lap, exhausted.

"Holy shit. Our plan worked. We made it. We *actually* made it."

The boat creaks steadily as Zone T grows smaller behind us, a shell of the hell it used to be—no longer a prison, but a graveyard of painful memories now put to rest.

Before us, morning starts to spill across the river, painting the waves with gold. Charon steers us into dawn, facing the sunrise with that smile still on his lips. I can't help leaning forward to kiss it.

"I love you," I whisper against his mouth. "Thank you for saving me. Then, and now."

He kisses me back tenderly, blue eyes shining as he leads us toward a future I never hoped to dream of.

Toward *home,* with my Ferryman at my side. The owner of my rotten soul.

Though death had tried to claim it first;

It was always his to keep.

The soil's stubborn beneath my hands, rocky and dry near the base of the lighthouse, but it gives eventually. Everything does, if you press hard enough. My fingers are blistered and caked with dirt when I lean back on my knees, examining the crosses we'd just finished erecting. They're crudely made, tied together with twine we found in the cellar, but they serve their purpose.

Two graves, side by side.

One for the woman who raised me, and one for the woman who raised *him.*

Charon leans against my side, quiet as always with his mother's book on his lap. The look on his face when he'd found it still in his nightstand will forever haunt me, the absolute relief that had sent him crashing to his knees.

"I'm sorry," I say, my voice barely a whisper against the ocean waves. "I know she...she killed your mom. She hurt you. She wasn't a good person."

His brow creases, but he shakes his head slowly, reaching out to rub the back of my neck. A shiver runs through me, and I close my eyes as I lose myself to the touch.

"I'm not burying the Judge, I'm burying my sister. The memory of her, anyway. Who she was before all of this."

Not that I have anything of hers to bury. Just the nightmares.

Nyx hops over, nudging my knuckles in a rare show of affection. I smile down at her sadly and gently stroke a finger down her beak.

Charon shifts beside me, his shoulder warm against mine. When I glance over, his eyes aren't on the graves anymore. They're on me.

The book lies open on his lap, a pressed flower caught between its pages, so delicate that it makes my throat ache. I reach for the nearest white stone, turning it in my palm before setting it atop the fresh mound of earth. "All of the pain we went through, all of the anger...it dies here."

He gently closes the book, setting it on the ground between us in order to pull his blade from his back pocket. I jolt in surprise when he presses the tip of the blade into his own fingertip, bright blood welling against his skin.

"Charon, what are you...?"

Lifting his hand, he starts to write on the wall above the graves, the blood smearing in deliberate strokes of letters I don't understand. When he leans back to meet my gaze, the marks glisten in the dying light.

Óso anapnéo

"What does it say?"

He grabs my hand and mouths softly into my palm, *"As long as I breathe."*

My heart skips a beat, thudding against my chest when he smiles against my skin, kissing it softly. Those words feel like a promise, not only for the dead, but the living as well. *Us.*

"As long as I breathe," I repeat—no, I *vow,* closing the gap between us to press my lips to his.

I don't know what our future may hold, or how long we can hang onto this life we've found, but I'm never letting go. There might come a day when he gets sick, or maybe I turn, and everything comes crashing down around us...but maybe the fear is supposed to be there. It'll remind us to never go back to where we were before. One foot forward at a time.

In my case, literally.

I never want Charon to hurt again, and I'll spend the rest of my days making him feel as safe and cherished as he's made me.

Until the end, whatever it takes, for as long as I can.

CHAPTER THIRTY-THREE

Charon

"**H**ey! Stay back, you thief."

The dock holds steady under my weight as I place down another board, smiling to myself when Hector curses Nyx for trying to steal from his pile of nails.

He's arguing with her between hammer swings, and she caws indignantly before fluttering just out of reach, the smug little menace.

Wiping sweat from my brow, I lower myself onto the sand where we keep our tools, stretching my sore legs out in front of me. We've been fixing the deck for a couple of weeks now, and it's nearly finished.

My shoulders ache, but it feels good. Before, the pain served as a reminder of a life condemned to the boat, but now...

Now it's proof of what we're building here.

"I swear, murder bird, if you nip my elbow one more time..."

Hector scoffs, glaring at Nyx with an annoyed mix of affection. My heart warms at the sight. Behind him, our lighthouse stands tall on the bluff, cracks in its foundation slowly being repaired. We've managed to barter supplies from a nearby outpost up the coast with the coins and bullets that the soldiers had forgotten to unload after dragging me away. I'm still amazed every day at our luck.

We'd tried to liberate Aster's Hollow from Lena's lies months ago, even going so far as to offer them half of our rations, but the fear ran too deep. They wouldn't listen to a rotter or a monster, still believing that someone would save them from the infection, so we'd left them to their own devices. Either they survive on their own...or they don't.

But we will.

A contented sigh leaves my lips as I reach beside me, pulling my mother's book from beneath a folded tarp. The pages are more fragile than ever, cover barely clinging to the spine. When we'd found it still tucked away inside my nightstand on the boat, I'd nearly wept. It's a miracle the thing has survived this long, and yet here it is. Still holding on, just like me.

Like us.

Hector tosses his hammer down, groaning as he pushes to his feet. "Alright, I'm done with this for now. It's time to check the traps."

He limps past, bending to kiss the top of my head on his way down to the shoreline where we keep our nets for catching fish. I drop my gaze to the prosthetic foot I'd made as soon as we'd gotten back from Zone T, pleased with how well he's walking now. It may be rudimentary in nature, whittled from wood and screws and old springs, but it gives him his range of motion back. Helping me fix up our home is his new favorite thing.

Absently, I trace the worn leather cover in my hands, my mind slipping to the epics buried within. Stories of war, wrath, and loss. Pages filled with profound grief. As I listen to Hector bicker with Nyx in the background, I know our story isn't like the ones inside these pages anymore.

This isn't a tragedy.

Our lighthouse that we've grown to love will probably never be perfect. Half the windows are gone, and the stairs to the top will take years to mend, but it's *ours*. We'll fix it piece by piece. We'll leave our mark here, in every board and beam, every part we make brand new.

This book might fall apart before we finish reading it.

But the life we're building—the one we chose, the one we bled for... that'll stay.

Just like these tattered pages and the photos Hector keeps on the wall, this place won't forget us, even if the rest of the world does. Not while our hands have touched it.

Not while our love lives on.

"We've got a good catch this morning," Hector says quietly, drawing me from my thoughts. I raise my gaze to find him standing above, emerald eyes searching my face. "I bet we could trade the fish for yeast or something. Learn how to bake bread. Or get some chickens."

He drops into my lap with a soft grunt, pulling my arms around his waist. Nyx lands at our feet a moment later, a small fish clamped in her beak.

"I mean, don't get me wrong, those stale crackers in the cellar aren't bad soaked in water, but I'd probably kill someone for scrambled eggs and toast."

I huff a laugh through my nose and offer him the book, running my palms over his newly muscled chest. He takes it carefully, turning it over in his hands as he stares down at the title.

The Iliad.

Slowly, as much as my throat will allow, I'm teaching him to read it with me—just a few words at a time.

"We should write our own someday," he murmurs, glancing at me sideways. "So no one ever forgets us."

A soft, shy smile pulls at his cheeks when I kiss him deeply, my heart so full it could implode.

"I'll never forget," I mouth against his lips, returning the smile he's gifted me.

Let the world move on. Let it crumble and rebuild a thousand times over, we'll still be here.

In the salt-soaked wood of the dock beneath our feet and the lighthouse walls we've patched with our own hands. In every kiss and every scar.

The pages may run out and our world might end, but for now...

Our story has just begun.

EPILOGUE

Nyx – Twenty Years Later

The wind rustles my feathers.

High above the clouds, I soar, feathers whispering in the breeze, mixing with the salt and sea.

Down below, my lighthouse waits, home to humans who are mine.

I circle once before angling toward the open window at the top, the one they leave open just for me.

"In we go."

The air inside is warm, touched by the scent of paper and thyme. They are where they always are—one in the chair with a book in his hand, the other sitting on his lap, both covered with soft cloth.

They look older now.

Hair silvered at the temples, slower in the way they move. Quiet, as usual, but words have long since lost their weight.

"Pretty eyes."

They do not look up when I speak, but the long haired one smiles, a faint twitch of fingers against the chair. They know that I am here.

I have flown this path for decades.

My wings do not tire, and my eyes do not dim. The infection in the rain made certain of that.

And so I endure, watching over them in the long stretch of years that would have taken me from the sky if not for what runs through my veins.

When the wind calls, I will answer—

but I will always return.

Tomorrow.

And the day after.

And the day after that.

I am the last to remember his voice, the human who gave me words and love when the world took it all from him. Until the one with pretty eyes gave it all back.

And while the wind still carries me, I will keep them in my sight.

For as long as I breathe.

AFTERWORD

They called him the Ferryman.

In ancient myth, Charon ferried souls of the dead across the river Styx into the underworld. Those deemed too wicked by the Judge, Minos, were sent to Tartarus, a prison of eternal punishment.

The Charon in my story did something else...he ferried someone out.

The Iliad is a tragedy. Hector was once the prince of Troy, killed by Achilles and dragged behind his chariot while the world mourned his loss. My Hector clawed his way out of darkness with bared teeth, still choosing love over rage despite every chance to become like the monsters who hurt him.

Whether Zone T is Tartarus or Troy...well, that's entirely up to you.

My beautiful readers, thank you so much for reading to the end. This story was never about perfect love or perfect people, and it certainly wasn't about heroes. Charon and Hector aren't saviors. They're broken boys who fought their way toward each other through blood and pain. Somehow, in the aftermath of a world that tried to tear them apart, they found something worth saving. And who could forget Nyx, our murder bird and goddess of the night?

Love, even the messy kind, leaves a mark. Maybe all any of us can hope for is to leave a mark that tells the world we were loved and that we mattered.

To anyone who's ever believed that their story had to end in tragedy because the world said so, it doesn't. Never forget that even lost souls can be found. You're the one steering the boat, and you have the power to change course.

"There is the heat of Love, the pulsing rush of Longing, the lover's whisper, irresistible—magic to make the sanest man go mad." – Homer, The Iliad.

Hold on to love like Charon, believe you deserve it like Hector. Because you do. Always.

For as long as I breathe,

CONTENT WARNING

- Non-con/dub-con

- Gore

- Body horror

- Mutilation (not between MCs)

- Violence (not between MCs)

- Murder

- Torture (not between MCs)

- Loss of limb

- On-page sexual assault

- Mentions of off-page childhood sexual assault

- Heavily implied cannibalism

- Sex on top of a dying body

- A jar of human eyeballs

- Odaxelagnia (arousal from biting or being bitten)

- Blood used as lube

THANK YOU

To my alpha reader, Rae, for always being cool. No really, you're the coolest and I can't compete.

My betas, I absolutely adore all of you! Anya, Bri, Sarra, and Bree, thank you so much!

Joe, as always, for as long as I breathe. I love you.

And of course, to the amazing authors in the collab, you all are amazing and I can't wait to have all our books on my shelf!

CHECK OUT THE SERIES

Books in the 1nf3ction series:

Ash on the Tongue by Lee McCormick
Rotten by Bree Wiley
Obliterated by N. Boeyer
All Your Days by Ali Woods
Call to the Devil by B. Ripley
King of Lies by H.L Day
The Dead Don't Talk by Rae Stone
Bad Blood by Lyla Dane
Eden Calling by Gwen Martin

ABOUT THE AUTHOR

I'm a US resident who can be found cuddled on the couch with my partner and our black cat, Norman Bates. Mostly, I'm a homebody but I do enjoy getting lost in the woods. I love romance, fantasy, science fiction, and every horror video game ever made. Rotten is my sixth publication.

Other works by me:

State of Us Series

Finding Delaware

Crossing Arizona

Loving Ohio

Standalones

Pretty Broken Doll

Nothing Left to Say, a poetry collection

Follow me on socials! Scan the QR code below for my author links: